T0198649

A Mixture of Thoughts

Filton Hebbard

iUniverse, Inc.
New York   Bloomington

A Mixture of Thoughts

iUniverse books may be ordered through booksellers or by contacting:

iUniverse
1663 Liberty Drive
Bloomington, IN 47403
www.iuniverse.com
1-800-Authors (1-800-288-4677)

Because of the dynamic nature of the Internet, any Web addresses or links contained in this book may have changed since publication and may no longer be valid. The views expressed in this work are solely those of the author and do not necessarily reflect the views of the publisher, and the publisher hereby disclaims any responsibility for them.

ISBN: 978-1-4401-5832-2 (sc)
ISBN: 978-1-4401-5833-9 (dj)
ISBN: 978-1-4401-5834-6 (ebk)

Printed in the United States of America

iUniverse rev. date: 8/20/2009

To my daughter

Simona

Acknowledgements

I must express my gratitude and sincere appreciation of the assistance extended to me by some wonderful friends:

Steve and Robyn Lavis

Sharon Everson

Gwen Harber

Charles Muller (literary agent supreme whom I have yet to meet in person.)

and Holly   (a guiding light)

Filton Hebbard

Contents

Contents

REMINISCING OR DOTAGE

The smallest of memories can sometimes live the longest of them all.

An old man sat looking back; back over the hills of time. We are born with a periscope in our minds, he thought. We can look over hills within us, the mountains we climbed, the valleys of despair that engulfed us before we managed to escape.

What was a mind? How did it store our memories? Were they side-by-side in the order of their happenings, or was there a place for the good and a place for the bad?

How many memories could a mind contain? The answer would have to be in the millions, but how many could one recall and record? An impossible task. They hid until we wanted them.

Strange place, the mind. As one grew older it changed its habits. No longer did it hoard the names of new acquaintances. It threw them out. Not worth keeping. But the acquaintances of childhood hung in there like glue.

Did the mind have a mind of its own? Did it tell the aged that there was no point in retaining the names of new acquaintances? Ashes-to-ashes and dust-to-dust. Soon it would all be a name on a crematorium wall or a plot of ground.

So why bother hoarding the names of new acquaintances whom one might never meet again, when the mind was stuffed full of those other memories of life, the years of life that had really been worth keeping?

Maybe the mind had sense and reasoning of its own, too?

No. I don't think so, he thought. Doubt had a say in that. The mind retained the rotten memories as well as the good. It stored the injustices as readily as it stored the kindness, the pleasures and the fun.

Funny, that way, too. One moment the mind was filling us with joy, the next moment it was reminding us of something that we desperately wanted to forget.

If it has the power to remember all of the things that we wanted to forget, why didn't it remember all of the things that were important to us? Like at school? Sometimes, even simple things didn't stick in our minds at all. It was as if part of it had a nasty streak. Like birthdays; your mums or your dads. They were more important than your own, in a way. If they didn't have birthdays, you wouldn't have even had a first birthday.

So let's reflect from the beginning, the old man said to himself; let's reflect from childhood.

They were pleasant times, those years before official school.

Mum teaching me how to tell the time and how to spell simple words like cat and dog. And giving me a biscuit with a hard lolly on the top if I got the spelling right. And giving me the same sort of biscuit for trying so hard if I got the spelling wrong! Sometimes Dad would sit me on his leg while he let me pretend that I was driving the car. I couldn't see over the

3

dashboard on those days, to say nothing of the road ahead, but I thought it was marvellous.

"Am I driving proper, Dad", I'd ask. And his reply, "Yes, son, as straight as a die".

A die? I never understood that remark, but it sounded good. Another beauty of childhood, that expression. If it sounded good it was acceptable.

Mum said.

Dad said.

It was the law.

"Eat your peas and beans, son, and you'll grow big and strong like Daddy".

"I want to grow up like you too, Mum."

"You'll never grow up like me, son. Not all over".

"Why? I want to".

"Well, son, what I want you to do is to eat your peas and beans, and when your older you'll know why you won't grow up like me".

Gee.

"You'll enjoy it, son, when you know the difference," Dad had cut in with a cheeky look in his eyes........." It's worth waiting for".

And a couple of years later; maybe six or seven years old; sitting out there behind the front fence to the yard; made out of galvanised roofing iron, that fence, as a mixture of blank privacy and protection from the dust that the unsealed road created.

Sitting with that girl of similar age whose mother was inside the house with my mother. Old school pals, or something, those mothers seemed to be.

There was just ordinary dirt where that girl and I were sitting, which was normal for kids in those early days in bush towns.

Well, what happened next, my memory won't forget if I live to turn about three hundred.

She pulled her dress up high enough for me to see her dirty pants. Most kids wore their underpants for a whole week at a time in those days. Water was expensive and fresh underpants came about on Mondays. Washing day for everything was Mondays. All in together like an Irish Stew.

Well, that's what Mum called it. Things were a bit different with boys, because underpants and outer pants were sewn together. The whole box and dice went into the Monday boil-up.

Anyhow, that's not what got a fixed place in my mind. Sitting there in the dirt by the front fence, this girl said.

"You show me yours, and I'll show you my fly-catcher".

My what?

Her fly-catcher.

What was she talking about?

Then she wiggled a bit, and pulled her pants down a few inches.

Boy, did I get a fright! Her dick had fallen off. All she had was a slit that a modern-day Visa card might fit into.

I stared and started to cry so she pulled her pants up.

I don't know whether I was crying because she'd lost her dick or whether I was scared the disease might be catching.

What did she hang on to when she went to the toily?

It was a few years later when one of my older brothers gave me the reality of the situation that I understood why Mum had said that I wouldn't grow up like her....... and it took a few more years to learn why Dad had said that I'd enjoy the reason when I learnt it.

Well. All I managed to do when I thought that little girl had lost her dick, was to run around to the back of the house, rub my wrists over the tears that were pouring down, and climb up a peppercorn tree.

A voice broke in on my thoughts. A voice I loved to hear. My daughter's.

"A cup of tea, Dad. Drink it while it's hot".

"Thanks, Sweetie".

Steam was coming off it. Too hot to drink at the moment.

What came next?

Starting school. Hanging on to Mum's hand as if I were sinking.

"Are you coming in too, Mum?"

"No. Not inside. I'll be here to meet you when you get out".

"Get out? Hell. Do they lock you up inside, Mum?"

"No. They teach you things".

"I don't want to learn any more things".

I had a mental picture of that girl with no dick.

"I know lots now, Mum. I can tell the time".

"Yes. After about three shots at it. Come on now. They're waiting. Be a little man".

"I don't want to be a little man. I want to be big like Daddy".

"Alright. But be a good boy. Here's the teacher coming".

"You're my teacher, Mum".

"At home I am. They teach you different things here".

"I don't want to learn different things".

I wanted to climb up another tree.

The teacher smiled. Her teeth were an inch long. She took my other hand. For the first time in my life, I wished I'd been born with one hand. The one Mum held.

But it ended up O.K, that first day.

The teacher didn't cut my finger off for sticking it up my nose or anything like that. I remembered what Dad had said once.

"If you keep sticking your finger up your nose, son, it might jam in there and I'll have to cut it off"

Jam in there! Hell. Did you have jam in your nose? Was that stuff you blew out really edible? Mine looked awful.

But hoorah. School work was easy. I was good at it

I was pretty good at football, cricket and swimming, too.

So life was O.K. Thanks, Mum.

And those older teenage years when girls' legs seemed to have magnets in them that kept dragging at your eyes.

And later still when you learned for certain why girls didn't have a dick.

"Dad, you've let your tea go cold. I'll get you another cup".

"Sorry, Sweetie, I've been day-dreaming".

"Day-dreaming? What have you got to dream about? Retired. Nothing to do but sit in the sun".

"Your turn will come, Sweetie".

"I'll get your tea".

"Thanks".

The mind sure was a strange place. It was a mystery world of its own. The things it store away then fished up for no apparent reason.

Like that comment of his daughter. What have you got to dream about?

If only she knew.

Plenty. That's what, Sweetie. Plenty.

Another funny thing about the mind. When you were young it looked to the future. It anticipated.

When you were old, it looked to the past. It reminisced.

What was the past? Wishing for something to occur and knowing it might never happen, or knowing that something you had wished for had occurred and knowing that it could never happen again, but that you could live with its memories.

Did you appreciate it more now than you had at the time of its occurrence?

Well. Too late to care. Its day was over. But it was good to have it as a memory. Somehow, it rode over the top of the rotten things that had kicked your shins.

"Here's your tea, Dad. Now drink it while it's hot. You used to say that drinking cold tea was a bit like sucking an old sock".

"Thanks, Sweetie. You're beautiful".

Did he ever truly say that about cold tea? He'd never sucked an old sock. An even if he'd sucked a new sock, it must have been a hell of a long time ago. So he couldn't have been growing old and stupid then.

Did you grow stupid when you were old?

Old and stupid? Not a fair expression, that one. True, you were slower than before, when you grew older, but were you stupid?

Old people don't call each other stupid. Well, not unless they were stupid themselves.

It was the young who made those sorts of remarks, and how could they know. They were still young, and age had reasons of its own.

How could anybody justify a decision on behaviour when they weren't old enough to have experienced the situation themselves?

Easy. Everybody did dopey things when they were young. Like boys walking along the top of a picket fence when the pickets were all waiting for their chance to say "got him, right up the dunger".

And parents. Parents were the source of all knowledge until their children got a few teenage years under their belt. Then parents suddenly became so wrong. So wrong, and out of touch with reality.

A sip of tea. Hell it was hot. Why did boiling water have to be so hot? The tea would have to wait a while.

Teenage years. What an embarrassing time that was in certain ways. Not so much in the first few years, but when you knew you were 'growing old'.

What happened then? Yes, you felt gawky when your dick started to grow bigger, but it was damned embarrassing when it released that sticky stuff into your pyjamas when you were asleep.

How could you hide that from your Mum when she did the weekly wash?

Did that happen to girls too? They'd never talk about it, if they did. Maybe they'd think they were taking a fit.

Really opposite, girls and boys, weren't they? Boys tried to look tough and manly in their teenage years, and girls tried to look sweet and sophisticated.

Both a bit dopey. Remember that song Judy Garland used to sing – 'I'm Just An In - between'? Very true.

Boys liked to swear. Now that was really grown up and tough.

"Don't use that 'F' word in the house", I heard the mother of one of my mates say.

But those more significant teenage things. Like that little girl who used to wait outside the Scout's Hall every Thursday night and walk homewards with about half a dozen of us kids in the thirteen to fourteen age group.

"Who wants to do it tonight"? she used to ask. "You all can if you want to".

7

I was sure she'd end up making a living on her back until I met her once when we were both in our mid-twenties.

It was one of those bumped-into-in-the-street situations. We both stared, stopped, looked around, then started to laugh.

"Not Rosalie"?

"Every bit of her, old school pal of mine. How are you?"

She was beautiful. Nicely dressed, hair groomed, mild lipstick, white teeth............. and two little impeccably dressed children.

We chatted for a while. No embarrassment. What a change. Any man would have been proud to call her his wife.

Married to a doctor, she was. It made me wonder how she'd met him. I was delighted for her. Kept on thinking about her for ages.

She didn't reveal any sense of guilt in that meeting of ours. Maybe she had more strength of character than I had myself.

But it was a lesson. I learnt a hell of a lot from that meeting with Rosalie. I don't know what it was that I learnt but it lifted me up a peg or two about life. How? Why? I don't know, but I did. I grew in the mind.

Life shapes some of us, and some of us shape life.

Who said that to me? Dad I think.

So what about life? I was about seventeen when my father asked me what I wanted to be in the future.

I was mad about motor bikes at the time, so I told the truth. " I don't know", I replied.

"You ought to study Law, son. Be a solicitor. You think and you think good. You don't always use them, but you have brains".

A solicitor! Hell. Did solicitors ride motor bikes? And brains? I'd read somewhere that brains shrink one percent each year. But the writer didn't say when the shrinking started. If it started as soon as you were born, by the time anybody reached a hundred they wouldn't have any brains left. Just a nut inside a nut.

Some people sure did write strange things. Imagine your brains shrinking. You'd have hollow spaces in your head. Swing your head around quickly and your brains would lurch the opposite way. Later on they'd hit the inner wall.

Did my daughter think that my brains were shrinking?

"I'll put that big, cane chair that you like out in the sun for you, Dad".

Maybe she did. I was perfectly capable of lifting that chair myself. A bit awkward, that's all. The cushions slid into the dirt now and then when I did it, I must admit.

"There you are", she'd say. "Nice and comfy. I'll get your hat for you. Must take care of that dear old nut for you".

To reflect on things and casually term your own head a nut was one thing, but to have one of the family give it the same title scarcely a half an hour later, was a bit worrisome.

Perhaps a bit of detailed thought about the years gone by ought to be considered. Pensive reflection.

Well. No trouble there. Was yesterday the shopping day or was it the day before? Did it matter? Of course it didn't matter. Yesterday was over and done with.

That girl who used to call around to the Scout Hall every Thursday night was as clear as daylight in the mind. And that was over fifty years ago. Hell.

Scouts was certainly a night to look forward to. You can all do it if you like. Wacko.

But what about Dad thinking I'd make a good solicitor. Well I had, hadn't I.

Just a lucky break in my life. If he'd suggested the Police Force I'd have been compelled to arrest myself.

So I became a solicitor. Great. Like I said earlier, I think school work and other general study was a milk run. But I had to get rid of the motor bike when Dad bought me a little car.

"Dignity, son", he'd said. "Dignity. You don't ride a horse without a saddle".

I never knew what he meant by that remark but I let it pass. You can't keep quoting your father when some of your examination results weren't too exciting.

Met my wife at University. Clicked if off from the beginning, we did. Coming to think of it, she used to suck queer lollies in those days. If she were young today she'd probably end up a junkie.

No complaint from me. Always affectionate, she was. Kept the house tidy.

Funny life being a solicitor. You made a good income, more from what you knew than what you did.

Better have another sip of that tea. Christ, it's cold! I wonder if it would taste that way if I drank it through an old sock? Fancy trying to drink it that way.

I'll chuck it out and pretend I drank it.

"I saw you toss your tea away, Dad. What was wrong with it"?

"A fly, Sweetie. I'm sorry. It drowned in it. Floating on the top".

"Yes, you silly devil. Didn't you know. Humans have to put their heads under water to drown. But flies are more clever than us. They drown on the surface without getting their heads wet".

We both laughed.

"I don't know if that's right or not, but do you have any more tea"?

"For you, anytime".

"Thanks, Sweetie".

I waited for the tea, sipped it, found it again too hot to drink, so I set it down.

Now, where was I.

Oh, yes, a young solicitor making fairly good money, married, with two lovely daughters. That was when I was younger of course.

Now, back to the mind.

Just think of all those records of basic living locked up in a person's mind. Kind of ridiculous. The work, the holidays, the mumps, the measles, the food we liked, the food we didn't like. Hell. Where was a person's memory anyhow? It had to be in your brains, of course. There didn't seem to be anything else in your head except your brains.

And if your brains shrank one percent a year, by the time you died you'd only have a pretty hollow sort of head to take to bed at night by the time of your retirement from daily work.

There must be something wrong with that equation.

So where was the sense in that shrinking bit, especially when an older person found it was easier to remember things that occurred as a child, rather than things that occurred ten years before now? Surely the first part of a brain that filled would end up on the bottom shelf and be the first squeezed out of the back door.

Or was it?

'They' reckon, I don't know who 'they' are, but they reckon that a large part of the brain has unknown duties. Someone has as accident and gets a wallop on the head that flattens part of his brain, and then comes out of a coma, seemingly untouched.

But was he untouched?

Was the squashed part simply storing away those little memories of ours that we thought we had forgotten?

Well, I don't know. But one of the really good things about growing old is your memory box. Where it is in your head, doesn't matter. It's in there somewhere.

It's yours alone, that memory box. You own it, you keep it or share it as you please. You laugh with some of it and you cry with other parts of it.

It's a gift. It's a precious book of your own. It's a book for you to read as often as you like, whenever you like, and nobody knows what chapter you're up to. It's a manuscript of massive dimensions.

You can improve on it with thoughts of what you'd do if you had it all over again. How you'd fill it, the sadness you'd avoid right from the earliest days.

Remember in school when the teacher made some of the boys sit with the girls in those twin desks. It was supposed to be punishment for not paying proper attention.

Miss Moore, that teacher's name was, so far as the pupils were concerned, but someone said she was married to a copper. A real, live copper, not one of those things your mother boiled the clothes in. A policeman. Big feet.

You were nervous, weren't you when you had to sit next to Jessie Brown?

She was cheeky, Jessie Brown. But nice. Not thinking, your hand rested on Jessie's bare thigh under the desk, and boy was it a thrill to remember.

Before you could pull your hand away, Jessie grabbed it and looking all innocent at the teacher, she plopped it slap-bang over her mickey and held it there.

Still comes back to me, that day. As clear as if it were right now, today, again.

I was shaking with I don't know what..............

"That's the third cup of tea and you've scarcely touched it, Dad. You'd better lose that silly grin and come inside out of the sun. I'll bet you were thinking of that day when they made you senior solicitor and there were about ten others in the firm with longer service".

"Yes. That was a nice day, Sweetie. But I will come inside. It was getting a bit hot out here, and I kept falling asleep".

"So, that's why you didn't drink your tea".

Dreams are beautiful when you're old. Got sense in them. Well, some of them. Like that little girl after Scouts. The one who grew up to be beautiful and great to talk to.

"Come on, Dad. Give me your hand and mind the step".

How could I give her my hand, I needed it.

And mind the step, she'd said.

How could I mind the step, it was part of the house.

It sure took young people a long time to get old-age sense.

"Hang on, Sweetie. You're walking too fast".

"Sorry".

"Have you got any of those cakes with the lolly on the top? The ones the kids like?"

"Yes, Dad. I always save a couple for you".

"They're yummy".

11

"Yes, Mum used to make them when Jessie and I were kids. She gave me the recipe".

"She was always kind. Like you are, Sweetie".

"We'll go up to the hospital to see her after lunch".

"Is it Sunday already?"

"No, it's Thursday".

"But I go up on Sundays. Lovely person, your mother. She's losing her marbles, you know. She asked me who I was last time".

"Yes, Dad, I know. I was there. It's dementia".

"Must be those lollies she sucks".

"What lollies?"

"I don't know. She offered me one when we first met. I spat it out".

"Dad, you met Mum over forty years ago, I'm forty three".

"Gee. Time sure flies. Why are we going to see her on a Thursday? You said it's Thursday".

"It's Mum's birthday".

"So, she's still having birthdays".

"Come on, Dad. Give me your hand".

"Only for a loan. I want it back".

Verses

Filton Hebbard

A HEAD ON A PILLOW

Don't you delay now, my lonely friend
The kindest of blessings to all I do send

It comes so easy, with evening bliss
A head on a pillow, someone to kiss

And I on my tip-toes, will leave your room
To dreamland dear sweethearts, a bride and a groom

You must not worry, or bother to care
For in your dreamland, I will be there

And now I do wish you, the fondest goodnight
And grant you true loving, throughout the night

So now he's departed, my friend Sandman Joe
I'll heed his message, to dreamland I'll go

Knowing my darling, it's there that I'll see
The gateway to heaven, for you and for me.

A LONELY ROAD

There's a lonely road before me
    and a lonely road behind
There's torment in my thinking
    that will not leave my mind
There are memories of loving
    that once were daily fare
And the emptiness of knowing
    that you're no longer there
My heart is slowly breaking
    as I recall so clear
The joy that filled my living
    when your laughter I could hear
But now that you're in heaven
    and I am all alone
I'll walk right through my future
    and do it on my own
For I cannot for a moment
    think of anyone but you
To share with me the loving
    the way that lovers do
And when my road has ended
    that road I walk along
I'll stretch my arms to reach you
    and my heart will fill with song
For I'll have joined a heaven
    that you once made for me
And we will live forever
    in that world no-one can see.

Filton Hebbard

A LOVER'S LIPS

I never seek an angel
    to hold within my arms

Or a picture book of beauty
    to dazzle me with charms

I simple seek a lover
    whom I know is ever true

To share with me the troubles
    that come as troubles do

And when we wake each morning
    to face another day

We'll do it full of sunshine
    even though the skies are grey

We'll laugh when we fall over
    having done a crazy thing

For life is full of tumbles
    in every wedding ring

But there is certain tonic
    in all kisses genuine

And the flavour of a lover's lips
    is more warming than good wine

So, darling let me find you
    wherever you may be

And the love I'll always give you
    will be my own ecstasy.

A PRINCESS

I wonder at the thinking,
Of this, our human race
When we turn our gaze from substance,
To admire frills and lace

We seem to think that protocol
Is nonsense to ignore,
Then criticise its absence,
Should it not reach the fore

We laud the Monarchy today,
And condemn it on the morrow,
Yet give no better reason than
It failed to weep in sorrow

When silent in its dignity,
If that is what we seek,
We protest in our anguish,
For we are maudlin weak

We say a princess may behave
In any way she chooses,
Then lift our voice to heaven
If Royalty she loses

It's true we should give credit
To the fine and noble task,
Of those who foster charities,
And never credit ask

But have we overlooked the fact
That justice isn't met,
Until the stories other side,
Is offered up to vet

For Monarchy is silent,
Bound by its old tradition,
While we are clambering to buy
The latest press edition

That press comes forth with headlines
About great love and care,
But has a mother ever lived,
Not feeling great despair

So let our British decency
Turn mirrors to each face,
And open up reality
To what we do embrace

This world of ours has lemon peel,
Unpleasant in its rind,
Yet we the ones who made it
Blame others, so unkind

How many adult tears are spilt
To be part of the throng,
When if that mirror answered back,
They'd not know right from wrong

There are ten thousand workers,
Unglamorous, good folk,
Who toil from dawn to night-fall
With charities their yoke

They do not turn for photographs,
Or have a cause to smile,
They simply get on with their job
Of making life worthwhile

So we should think with fairness,
When we are casting stones,
Least we be guilty of the crime
Of breaking kinder bones

And a prouder man I'd be this day,
Coursed with my British blood,
If I were sure my kinsfolk
Could climb out from the mud.

A SPECIAL BREED

They were a special breed of man
    those early pioneers
Some of them had reached eventide
    and some of tender years

They searched the hills and lowlands
    for that most elusive gold
And when the day closed down to night
    their stories did unfold

They shared a type of friendship
    from the common bond of pain
Where the sun burnt from the heavens
    and the clouds forgot to rain

They picked the earth and shovelled
    and wiped that sweaty face
Then in the morning drank sweet tea
    with thoughts of frills and lace

They spoke of families left behind
    and better days to come
But deep within their aching hearts
    they knew you can't fool some

They welcomed strangers passing by
    to share their scanty meal
For helping is religion
    when you know how others feel

They talked about the only things
    that they could talk about
Like when a stripling little kid
    took on a drunken lout

They cherished female tenderness
    a woman's kindly ways
Yet boasted of a girl they knew
    who handled bullock drays

Filton Hebbard

They never looked for sympathy
    when Lady Luck was down
They simply hoped their missus could
    hold up her head in town

They were the salt of this good earth
    those early pioneers
And if you live in comfort now
    give them three hearty cheers

For they made this fine country
    the land of which we're proud
The basis of the backbone
    that makes us cry out loud

We'll fight you if we have to
    or love you if we can
We'll offer hands of greeting
    be you woman or a man

We'll share with you our foodstuffs
    and pass the time of day
But never get the feeling
    that we don't know our way

For deep within the makings
    of the good Australian breed
Is a little bit of Grandpa
    and that pioneers creed

We'll meet you on the playing fields
    or anywhere you please
But if you dare to hurt our mates
    we'll bring you to your knees

For we have felt the hardship
    of living off the land
And the need to show the birthright
    of an offered friendly hand

So steady with the stockwhip
    those days have long gone past
No matter whether forebears
    saw gallows or the mast

Just face the world with courage
    front everything that shows
And if you have to lose a few
    well that's the way it goes

For there must be a heaven
    for the woman and the man
Who treat the world around them
    in the best way that they can.

Filton Hebbard

A TROUBLED JOURNEY

Life is a troubled journey
    through trust in fellow man,
For mostly they will use us
    in any way they can,
They smile each time they greet us
    their handshake firm and strong,
They stand beside us in the bar
    their friendship lyrics long,
But when an issue arises
    where accolades abound,
If they can climb upon your back
    that's where they'll be found,
But I met you, dear Neville,
    way back in seventy two,
I sought a job as manager
    with you to interview,
And as the years rolled slowly by
    our friendship stood rock-firm,
Not once did it see tatters
    not once did it adjourn,
I saw you in the thinking
    that longed to find goodwill,
In every fellow man you met
    and I can see it still,
You did not seek the banner
    to wave it at a crowd,
Your voice was ever gentle
    it never shrieked out loud,
Whenever I did blunder
    and needed a staunch friend,
I always found you near me
    to help me make amend,
And now that you are ninety
    with ten more years to go,
I feel that I've been lucky
    a true friend I still know.

A WOMAN'S MIND

He tried to search a woman's mind
The strangest mystery there to find
But even though he fathomed deep
Their secrets they alone could keep
For women could not justly claim
They knew the end to nature's game
They laughed sometimes before they cried
And that was when they often lied

They lied from wish to form a shield
Lest prying thoughts their errors yield
For women have the painful task
Of trusting men who wear a mask
And this mask is not decency
It hides deep urge for ecstasy
But when it comes with its veneer
Soft women sometimes it endear

And should they find at later date
When they have taken it to mate
That it was thinking quite unreal
A surging anger they will feel
And they will turn upon a friend
Who only wanted to amend
By opening the sincere arms
That offer strength devoid of charms

And when a word put here or there
Should indicate this world unfair
They flame within their woman's mind
And ooze a bitterness unkind
For they stand high with heady might
To exercise God's given right
For them to choose their own sweet path
Regardless of shame's aftermath

And they do this the whole world wide
Before or after they have cried
For when their mind is anger swept
Its grasp on living is inept
And they see fault in everything
From kindest words to wedding ring
And man must shrug and say goodnight
With hopes that one day they'll see light

For man does hate to criticise
A past behaviour not so wise
Of someone very dear to him
Who might have fallen to loose whim
Though decent man will feel the need
To pass on knowledge of his creed
For women rarely ever know
The one with whom they altar go

And even though they claim the right
To chose their partner in the night
They'd feel so better many times
And sugars wouldn't turn to limes
If sometimes they would lend an ear
To take in words from one quite near
Who couldn't reach that woman's mind
For answers there no man can find.

A WOMAN'S MOODS

Sweet little girl
What stirs your mind
Why are you of mixed passions
A balance you can't find

Today your voice is warm
There's feeling everywhere
Without the slightest doubting
One knows you really care

Then tomorrow
Or maybe yesterday
There is a certain distance
A coldness you display

No reason ever given
The change is not explained
Have you been disillusioned
Has hurt upon you rained

You show a feeling
A substance very real
Then suddenly you chill it
You take it from the deal

Are you afraid
If so where is your fear
Do you mistrust yourself
Or one who loves so dear

Time passes by
It suffers not in doubt
But you are spending conscience
Whilst life dims slowly out.

Filton Hebbard

AMBITION

The times were slowly changing
She looked back through the years
Faint cries in life's great wilderness
Had echoes moist with tears

For who knows of the future
Are changes for the best
At least we know what we have got
When it's right there to test

And our sweet little lady
Changed no-one but herself
The love she felt now for one man
Kept her on spinsters shelf

For she did see her anger
Her urge to vent her ire
As something in a parallel
To moods that flame like fire

For one man on a dais
He too with big ideas
Had torn the world to pieces
And caused ten million fears

And life from gentle thinking
She knew was for the best
To let it just drift slowly by
Brought slumber sound in rest.

AN ENIGMA   Young Man,   Young Maid

I'll give you love, the young man said
    if you, dear maid, will share my bed
My kisses flow as pure as wine
    with passion that is sheer divine

For me to lie within your bed
    the young maid with compassion said
I'd have to think that life divine
    was found elsewhere than in your wine

Oh, no, dear maid, you read me wrong
    my heart beats with the sweetest song
I'll touch you with and angel's care
    from tiny toes to shining hair

Oh, yes, young man, I know your song
    so let me think that I'm not wrong
You'd love to touch my shining hair
    but most young maids don't leave it there.

Filton Hebbard

AN EVIL IN THIS WORLD

There is an evil in the world
And it is the devil's brew
It sullies decent thinking
And adds it to the stew

It is an unknown factor
That works upon each mind
It culls our conversations
For hate in there to find

It magnifies our simple words
The things we said in fun
And after some dissection
It's a bullet and a gun

It makes us mistrust honesty
We look for reasons why
Someone showed us a kindness
Does the ointment hold a fly

It's true we must be cautious
Rogues fleece us if they can
And rogues have operated
Since the day that life began

But there is evil rampant
The type we can't define
It simply crumbles friendships
And makes fond love repine.

AN OLD MAN IN A FARMHOUSE

There's an old man in a farmhouse
    not very far from you
Who tells a lot of stories
    and all of them are true
He'll talk to you of loving
    and the horror of all wars
To the joy of family living
    with its countless daily chores
He's sure to mention many friends
    and games he used to play
When he was still a youngster
    and sports filled half the day
He'll get to speak of study
    with the need to form a life
That makes success of marriage
    when a man takes on a wife
But when he touches on that point
    you'll hear a softer tone
And his eyes will half-close misty
    as if he's all alone
It seems as if a happening
    back somewhere in those years
Has caused him an injustice
    an inner flood of tears
But though he never talks of it
    you cannot help but see
He hopes it doesn't happen
    to the likes of you or me
For emotion has a memory
    built on a clinging vine
Not only does it haunt us
    it magnifies in wine
But all our lives are subject
    to the good things and the bad
And the joy in those around us
    softens lost loves that are sad
So we are forced to swallow
    life's common bitter pill
And the old man in the farmhouse

knows that pain is never still
So if you seek a heaven
    to call your very own
The daily flowers that you'll see
    are the ones that you have sown.

AS A MAN

I was walking all lonesome
    down by the wide river
When the girl of my dreams
    I did see
She was sitting and gazing
    across that blue water
With not even a glance
    at poor me
I stood looking and waiting
    as if I were dumbstruck
Too frightened to move
    or to say
May I sit down beside you
    and promise to love you
For all of my life
    plus a day
But while I was planning
    on how to approach her
She rose to her feet
    with true style
Then dusted her hands
    as if with decision
While I couldn't conjure
    a smile
But with a quick movement
    she jumped into the river
And vanished from out
    of my sight
And my gasp of horror
    was all I could offer
It's a sound that returns
    every night
So now I go walking
    down by that wide river
With a pain in my heart
    that is real
For that swift running water
    where I spent my childhood
The love of my dreams

    it did steal
But I know that river
    cannot be forsaken
For the hurt that has entered
    my life
For if I'd had the courage
    to plunge into that water
As a man I might now
    have a wife
As a man I might now have a wife.

CHRISTMAS

It's not for me to say
    as we pass through every day
That there ought to be
    a better kind of life

For the anguish that we bear
    that is here and everywhere
Is surely no man's wish
    for child or wife

And no matter how we try
    to avoid the urge to cry
There is always something
    hiding in the dark

But as the years roll by
    with great clouds in the sky
It's so great to lift that calendar
    and mark – a very special mark – to Christmas

I love to hear the sound of Christmas
    the laughter in my mother's voice
The thrill I always feel at Christmas
    when it comes to be my choice

I love to sense the joy of Christmas
    the tinsel dancing in the hall
The smiles that seem so full at Christmas
    when from the door there comes another call

I love the mood that goes with Christmas
    the merriness right there at every turn
I love the human need at Christmas
    when everybody has a special yearn

I love to feel the world at Christmas
    is celebrating for a common cause
And if we crossed hands at Christmas
    the human race would look ahead and pause

Though it's not for me to say
    as we pass through every day
That there ought to be
    a better kind of life

But as those years roll by
    with those grey clouds in the sky
It's so great to lift that calendar
    and mark – a very special mark – to Christmas.

COME BACK LITTLE DARLING

Love me, little darling
    I want to be true
Love me, little darling
    the way I love you

Think of those moments
    when we were alone
Think of those moments
    when you were my own

Forgive me for hurting
    the words that I said
Forgive me for hurting
    or I'd rather be dead

My poor heart is crying
    I've broken the rule
My poor heart is crying
    I've been such a fool

Come back, little darling
    return to me please
Come back, little darling
    I'm down on........
        down on my knees.

Filton Hebbard

COME DARLING

Come darling, come darling to me

I will give you, every little thing
First of all, the nicest golden ring
Then it's only loving that you'll see
My poor heart, will nevermore be free

Come darling, come darling, to me

We will build, a cosy little home
I will promise, that I'll never roam
If you give me, your tender hand
I'll give you a love that's ever grand

Come darling, come darling, to me

We'll have children, maybe two or three
A girl for you, perhaps a boy for me
We'll teach them, the proper way to live
They must learn, it's love we have to give

Come darling, come darling, to me

I will kiss, your lips so cherry red
Every night, as we lay warm in bed
I will say, they taste like sweetest wine
Then you'll know, that everything's fine

Come darling, come darling to me

When we're old, and hair has turned gray
I'll love you, the way I do today
Hold you close, is what I'll do
Feel the thrill, that is forever true

So come darling, come darling, to me.

COMPANY

I was walking one day through the village
As lonely as lonely could be
When I saw a stranger from heaven
Or that's how that girl seemed to me

I looked up above for a reason
Why was she there seated alone
Her beauty set my heart a-racing
Did I have a chance, it to own

She gave a sweet smile as I passed her
So I turned and asked could I stay
She glanced at the seat there beside her
And heaven was mine from that day

Now the message I send to young lovers
Is don't be afraid of the world
It is open for all who would use it
Not a mystery tied and unfurled

So if you're alone and you're lonely
There are others who feel the same way
Don't walk in a crowd to find company
It's around, anywhere, and day.

DARK IS THE NIGHT

Dark is the night
When there's no love around
When there cannot be found
Two gentle hands
That clasp as couples walk
Their hearts beating the talk
Of golden bands

Dark is the night
When there's no moon above
When there's no light of love
Beneath the sky
To show each lonely soul
That it should reach its goal
No reason why

Dark is the night
When courting has no place
When love has lost the race
Of tender things
That used to mean so much
The thrill as fingers touch
On wedding rings

Dark is the night
When we have closed the door
When love is never more
Gone with time
That took the joy from life
As man searched for a wife
With hearts in rhyme

Dark is the night
When there is not a dawn
When skies are so forlorn
That we decide
There is no need to care
Of treasures once called rare
To groom and bride

So there must never be
A time for you and me
When dark is the night.

Filton Hebbard

DARKNESS I SHARE ALONE

I've given my life all I could give it
    all that my freedom allowed
I've given my heart to you, sweetheart
    with a love that made me so proud

I've climbed up the stairway to heaven
    and fallen down stairs that were steep
I've suffered the torments of passion
    as I've tossed and turned in my sleep

But now that we've parted I wonder
    is heaven as sweet as they say
I had always thought it as a kingdom
    and night-time the prince of the day

So I sit in the shadow of darkness
    that once was a light of our own
And I know that tomorrow's bright sunshine
    will be darkness that I share alone.

DARLING

My darling how I love you
    please say that you'll be mine
I'll toast you with everything
    from my heart with sweetest wine

I'll give you all my treasures
    the things that meant so much
But they lose all their values
    when your gentle fingers touch

And with my arms around you
    there's nothing I declare
Could ever beat the feeling
    of knowing you are there

Your lips are sweet and tender
    your smile is angel blessed
Is that enough to please you
    or should I say the rest

Your figure is so shapely
    your walk so straight and true
There's pride and self assurance
    in everything you do

You never look at other men
    though they all look at you
And I sense when we pass them
    they wished they wore my shoe.

DEAR SWEET ANGELIC CHILD

Angelic was the winsome child
Or so her parents said
Soft golden locks curled to her nape
And tumbled o'er her head

Her eyes were blue and sparkling
Her nose a shape divine
Her skin rich cream of freshness
Her cheeks dipped in pale wine

Straight. slim and true her figure
Sweet laugh like tinkling stream
No sign she gave of anger
Not in the wildest dream

But she did take the baby boy
Not yet full six months old
And without tear or temper shown
Did bare him to the cold

The milk intended for this babe
She warmed and drank herself
Then washed the bottle spotless clean
And placed it on the shelf

Her parents stared in shocked dismay
At stiff and frozen mite
Long dead beyond recovery
Blue skin that once was white

But that dear sweet angelic child
Was happy with her toys
At school they pushed and tumbled her
Those dreadful freckled boys.

DID ANYBODY TELL YOU

Did anybody tell you
    you are sweeter than the rose
That blossoms in
    the early days of Spring

Did anybody tell you
    you are sure to be the reason
Why robins get that
    lovely urge to sing

Did anybody tell you
    you are warmer than the sun
That comes to turn away
    the Winter chill

Did anybody tell you
    you are cuddlier than kittens
For you could give them
    lessons at your will

Did anybody tell you
    you are blessed with understanding
And your kindness makes
    an angry man a fool

Did anybody tell you
    you are what I've always longed for
A sweetheart who plays loving
    by the rule

And the rule is that you cannot
    have two loved ones on a string
And the rule is that you
    cannot tell a lie

And the rule tells me sweetheart
    that I want to hold you closer
Please tell me that's your ruling
    till I die.

DOWN IN THE VALLEY

Down in the valley where the air is pure
Where the grass is green and troubles fewer
That's where I long to live all my days
And give my heart freedom to write many plays

Down in the valley where the water is sweet
Where my fingers stretch out to the love whom I meet
That's where my life shares a journey divine
And my pulse rate is pumping as if blood were wine

Down in the valley where the world seems lost
Where I'll live to the fullest without any cost
That's where I'll lie near the swift running stream
And know that I've finally found my own dream

Down in the valley where my cabin is old
Where its structure is wooden, both humble and old
That's where I'll die in the wisdom of peace
And my pains and my passions have found their release.

DREAMING II

I saw the sweetness on her lips
The laughter in her eyes

The fragrance that surrounded her
The scent where heaven lies

I saw my good friend look at her
His thoughts were ever clear

The passion that was drawing him
Was lost but very near

His eyes ran o'er that shapely frame
Quite small, but trim and true

The urge to take her in his arms
Was what he had to do

She slowly turned to greet him
Welcome in her smile

The thoughts they shared were mutual
She knew he'd stay a while

And as I turned with lonely heart
To walk out in the street

I wished that somehow, sometime soon
That kind of love I'd meet.

DREAMING AGAIN

Dreaming of you sweetheart
    that's what I always do
Turning on my pillow
    to wish the whole night through
Wonder what you're doing
    asleep or still awake
Reflecting on those moments
    of a love that we forsake
For you have lost your freedom
    there's nothing you can do
And I can only hold you
    in dreams that are not true
But if there is a heaven
    up in that pale clue sky
Please, darling, when I reach it
    say in my arms you'll lie
So I'll just keep on dreaming
    the way I always do
Turning on my pillow
    to wish the whole night through.

DREAMING IS A HABIT

Dreaming is a habit
    that will not pass me by
Listen when I'm sleeping
    you're sure to hear me sigh
I know I must be crazy
    to think I had a chance
To even be your partner
    in a make-believer's dance
Flirting with the shadows
    is all that I can do
Pretending I am kissing
    just no-one else but you
But when I get to heaven
    that's when I fall asleep
Nobody has the right to claim
    a love I want to keep
So I'll continue dreaming
    that seems all I can do
Till darling I awaken
    and find you're dreaming too.

Filton Hebbard

EVERMORE

From birth we work our way through life
    dreaming, planning, cursing strife

Feeling pain and bearing it
    until on Judgement Day we sit

To face a future ever more
    in anguish or in gentle score

And all because within our creed
    the doctrine says there is a need

To justify the things we do
    if endless peace we wish to woo

But if this Lord whose realm we long
    is truly made of arm so strong

Why could He not just build us better
    and cast us free from torments fetter.

EVERY LIVING SOUL

Each night when sun has fallen
I hear my lonely heart
It cries to me for someone
To meet and never part

And in my cold, cold room
When lights are turned down low
I think of all my feelings
For one I've yet to know

How cruel the world around us
To me it always seems
No matter where I find you
You're only in my dreams

But darling I'll be waiting
Forever till we meet
And when I gently touch you
My heart will pound a beat

For I know you are somewhere
That you belong to me
And I shall keep on waiting
Till in my arms you'll be

And when that sun has fallen
No longer will my heart
Cry out to me for someone
For we shall never part.

Filton Hebbard

FACING REALITY

Not always should we struggle
    for joys of heart and mind
Sometimes we reach a limit
    to what we hoped to find
And though we haven't lost our faith
    in love or other goal
It's just that we must analyse
    and seek another role

For wanting something badly
    from work to fondest play
Can take so much of effort
    before there comes the day
When stark amongst the greenery
    there is the darkest sign
And we read on it clearly
    give up or ever pine

No matter how it hurts us
    to cast aside fond hope
The power of man's thinking
    has greater strength than rope
And when our thoughts do tell us
    that we have lost a race
No matter how we feel the pain
    we must bow out with grace.

FOOD FOR THOUGHT

They got to arguing one night
    on what was food for thought
They both agreed that thinking
    was something next to naught

How could a thought need tucker
    the fellow pondered on
As he did scratch his bony head
    and buttered up a scone

His missus didn't help him much
    as she looked at his plate
He had a ceaseless appetite
    her god-forsaken mate

If thoughts are in your stomach
    she said to him at last
That saying has some merit
    they're fond of their repast

But if the thinking that they mean
    is stuck up in your head
Your thoughts don't need no tucker
    the poor old thing are dead.

Filton Hebbard

FORGET ME NOT

She was bent and stooped,
    she was old
The grey of her hair,
    streaked with gold
She shuffled the pathway,
    a cane tightly held
And compassion to help her,
    within me soon welled
Why was she out shopping,
    in that busy mall
The rush crowd of Christmas,
    might cause her to fall
My thoughts saw her sitting,
    in a lonely, dark room
With her plans for the future,
    a chasm of gloom
But as I drew closer,
    I could scarcely believe
The song she was singing,
    was hard to conceive
Her voice was quite tiny,
    to match her small frame
But the smile on her lips,
    said she knew an old game
With the sweetness of pleasure,
    and twinkle of eye
She sang -------- let's do it darling
    once more 'fore I die.

FRIENDSHIP

We walk alone, though we're together
We see the world, in different ways
It seems so great, to have a friendship
To hold it close, and hope it stays

There is no answer, to why we love it
It's like a food, we long for more
It's part of us, yet we don't trust it
It's in and out, a swinging door

What kind of life, would pass without it
Hot Summer days, would be so cold
The Winter rains, would douse our laughter
And suddenly, we'd feel so old

If we lose one, we seek another
Our lives seem lost, without a friend
For man is empty, his soul is void
If he's alone, when he meets the end.

Filton Hebbard

GENES?

What fear the little bee must have
     to give its sting then die
It makes me think of Flanders Field
     where soldiers in their thousands lie

They each had duties to perform
     to protect their King or Queen
And life to them took second place
     where honour must be seen

To lose one's life in self defence
     is clear and natural right
But losing it as duty bound
     gives rise to darker light

What is this instinct in a mind
     that says what we must do
If we walk proud within ourselves
     and wear a sturdy shoe

Could it be something in our blood
     the reason for our birth
Where the masses give protection
     to those of national worth

It isn't common in all life
     this strange protective mode
Cats scramble from a barking dog
     and fireworks, horses goad

I wonder if a special gene
     for scientists yet to find
Is lurking in captivity
     in a very privileged mind

But I will die still thinking
     of the strange sequence in life
Where men follow men as soldiers
     and die for another's strife.

GEORGIA II

I can't get Georgia------- off my mind
No matter where I chance----------- to be
Sunshine on the water brings back memories
Of Georgia------------------- and me

To see those dancing diamonds
Moving with the tide
I bubbled with emotion
We laughed and then we cried

It was so exciting
Talking of our love
As if we thought a blessing
Had fallen from Above

Holding hands together
Kissing in the park
Wishing it was night-time
Like lovers in the dark

A smile to greet the morning
A cuddle in the night
The warmth of true emotion
Of bodies close and tight

Climbing on that rainbow
That led towards the sky
Wondering if heaven
Was up---------- or where we lie

Oh, Georgia, how you hurt me
When you chose to walk away
I had so much been planning
For a happy wedding day

Did you think I was deceitful
With those sweet things that I said
But all the words I uttered
Came from my giddy head

I wanted to be near you
Through every night and day
I truly am not lying
When to the world I say

I can't get Georgia------------- off my mind
No matter where I chance------- to be
Sunshine on the water brings back memories
Of Georgia--------------------- and me.

GOD

What is this man called God
Up where green pastures grow
He is the most elusive kind
That fact we all do know

He must be of our flesh and blood
Young Jesus was his son
And that man down from curly hair
Looked just like anyone

He placed us on this earth they say
From scriptures we are told
And left us there with shortened life
While he grew very old

Now scientists tell us that our earth
Goes back a long, long way
So could there be the slightest chance
That God has had his day

He never pays a visit
Doesn't call at Christmas time
To join the celebrations
And toast his son with wine

It doesn't seem to bother him
That Allah has emerged
To place a claim on destiny
And with great speed has surged

So now we all should ask ourselves
Was Jesus what we thought
Or was he simply very much
Within a passion caught

To remedy the evil things
Wrapped in his fellow man
And chose to claim his father was
The source how life began

For God or Allah, take your pick
Might truly be the means
For wise old men of yesteryear
To patch the broken seams

Of what they saw around them
Good people running wild
And much in need of one strong hand
To treat them as a child.

GOING AWAY

I'm thinking of going away
Where the sky's always blue
And all lovers so true
Where the shadows they say
Are transparent not gray
I'm thinking of going away

I'm thinking of going away
Where the things that go wrong
Are all cured with a song
And sweet music and rhyme
Are simply there all the time
I'm thinking of going away

I'm thinking of dreaming again
I'm thinking of dreaming again
I'm thinking of dreaming
I'm sure I'm just dreaming
Just dreaming, just dreaming again.

GOODBYE TOMORROW WELCOME YESTERDAY

Someone said the Sun exploded
By a natural bomb all power loaded
To then create this rounded Earth
As it settled back to what it's worth

For such an act to happen here
There would be signs quite far and near
Fragments deep beneath the soil
Which we'd acclaim much more than oil

But maybe sometime years ahead
When all of us are truly dead
A new, new race born from our rubble
Will with excitement cause a bubble

And staring with their one big eye
Find evidence of how worlds die
For we have moved with greater speed
Than one would think to be a need

Seems only yesterday at school
When history was made a fool
And Robin Hood not long ago
Performed great deeds with simple bow

When we would travel miles to where
A flimsy bi-plane took the air
And motor cars of racing breed
Could reach a hundred at full speed

But now computers tell us how
To get more milk out of a cow
And men go up to fool around
A few months journey from the ground

Though with advancement of this kind
Have we improved the human mind

Our needs are greater it would seem
From humble pie to high esteem

Our neighbours trust us less and less
And we, of course, say it's their mess
If they aren't careful they'll regret
Let no man dare to kick our pet

So while we sit in smug repose
And armament around us grows
Our anger quickly comes unstable
If that guy coughs he'll learn who's able

Have we learnt much since Robin Hood
Who shot them through to do some good
Or shall five hundred years from now
Someone unearth an iron cow

For with our smart technology
We've grown so blind we cannot see
That the quicker we consume our wealth
We'll draw the curtain on our health

For the earth is not an endless cup
Limits own what it gives up
It feeds the rich and it feeds the poor
But its heart won't last forever more.

Filton Hebbard

HEAVEN

I stand on the hill of my childhood
    and look at the scene down below
I search through my treasure of memories
    with thoughts of how quick life can go

My eyes see the shattered stone buildings
    but my mind sees green pastures and peace
For my home is now remnants of bombing
    and the pain in my heart will not cease

I think of those childhood ambitions
    when I played in those lush verdant fields
Without a grey thought of tomorrow
    and the agony that it reveals

My heart fills with tears and emotions
    why does a man act like a fool
The wars that he fought in his childhood
    were just games with a neighbouring school

So I walk slowly down to the rubble
    and stand unabashed as I cried
It isn't the scene of my childhood
    It's the place where my wife and son died

And I know that I'll never recover
    to seek out what living is worth
For what is the value in heaven
    if our Lord lets us bomb it on earth.

HEAVEN II

The smile she gave was heaven
    when I passed her in the street
It conveyed to me a happiness
    and a world we all should greet

She was no more than nine or ten
    her movements lithe and swift
And I within my aging years
    did feel my thoughts uplift

Why was it that the joy of life
    did slowly pass us by
As troubles that beset us
    at times seemed mountain high

But the message from that smiling child
    to me was very sound
As the answers to mans' troubles
    was in wisdom he'd not found

For the happy days of childhood
    were without the urge to fame
And to climb an endless ladder
    made pride a losers game

And the thing they call ambition
    can at times be just so wrong
If it destroys your laughter
    and life has lost its song.

Filton Hebbard

HEAVEN OR NOT

The young man wept
Why do you cry the old man said
The young man wiped a soiled face
My dear Papa has fallen dead

And you did love him very much
Oh yes, I did the young man cried
He filled my room with many books
I look at them and know he's died

No, no young man, the old man said
You'll see his face on every page
And in your memory he'll appear
To feel your love and never age

The young man wiped his teary eyes
But you kind man are old and gray
How will your children think of you
When you have reached that awful day

The old man wept
Why do you cry the young man said
The old man wiped a wrinkled face
In Wars my two dear boys fell dead

And you did love them very much
Oh yes, I did the old man cried
I filled their rooms with many books
I look at them and know they've died

No, no old man, the young man said
You see their names each opening page
And in your memory they'll seem
All proudly at enlistment age

The old man wiped his teary eyes
But you are still with youthful strength
Soft words are kindness I'll agree
But I've had my pain in life's full length

The young man offered one soft hand
His teary eyes no longer wet
What you have suffered dear old man
My broken heart has still to get

The old man took the offered hand
Then forced a gentle smile
You've moved an inch in your young life
But I have moved a mile

If we to heaven one day go
With luck we'll not feel pain
But would we ask each other
If we'd choose life's trip again

Then the young man wrapped his arms around
The old man who was wise
And tears of maybe joy or pain
Flowed from each others eyes.

HERITAGE

Heritage, the background of the man
 and reason why I protest strong
My forebears came from England
 where history is long
But you, the rest of you
 who sit upon the rails
No matter what your colour be
 you know what life entails
Is there not deep-rooted yen
 to lift your head up high
And say with pride and dignity
 that's where my forebears lie
You cannot view their funeral pyre
 their ashes, niche or plot
For they are over distant shores
 their name you have forgot
But should you shout 'Republic'
 as if they do not rate
To please a man in politics
 who talks of Head of State
What benefit is it to you
 to throw aside your past
And fill the ego of a few
 who long to climb the mast
Now who shall be this Head of State
 someone you voted for?
Or could he be from Cabinet
 whose memory you abhor
Would you be justly proud right then
 for having voted, Yes?
When all you'd gained in doing so
 was another bout of stress
This land was built from courage
 from ancient fighting stock
But now Republicans would like
 our very soul to hock
I say the answer must be No
 we all are doing fine

Australia is a nation fine
   I toast it now with wine.

Filton Hebbard

HIND SIGHT

Comes a time to sit and wonder
At the loving we have done
On the pain and sometimes suffering
Of the madness and the fun

For memories control us
They tell us what to do
But how can we believe them
When love keeps shining through

We ask ourselves the question
Have we learnt from the past
Should our hearts stay in a prison
And our futures fly half-mast

How much of life is living
What chances lie ahead
Can we count on tomorrow
Or just live today instead

There is no easy answer
No prayer book quite complete
The lessons in our memories
Sometimes we all repeat

So if there is a pardon
To the thinking we all do
Let's reprimand our memories
And love like lovers true.

HIPPIES

Seek not the fortune of pure gold
Seek not the wealth of kings
Seek not thy neighbours' pastures
Seek not with greed for things

Seek health and joy of living
Seek love of fellow man
Seek smiles and ready laughter
Seek friendship if you can

Seek all that said the hippy
Seek sunshine every day
Seek everything for nothing
Seek music as you play

Seek freedom from all hardship
Seek other sweet life too
Seek fields of pretty flowers
Seek bed-mates fond of woo.

Filton Hebbard

HOLD ME TENDER

Hold me tender
Hug me tight
Touch me gently
Through the night

Kiss my lips
Caress my hair
Tell me always
You'll be there

Call me honey
Call me love
Be my heart
Sent from above

Tell the world
Tell everyone
I'm your moonlight
I'm your sun

For if you truly
Do that thing
My very soul
Will start to sing

And if you're honest
If you care
I'll go with you
Just anywhere

For what I'm asking
You to do
Is what I'd long
To do for you

A sweetheart you're
A world of fun
Just call to me
And I'll run, run, run

So---------
Hold me tender
Hug me tight
Touch me gently
Through the night

Kiss my lips
Caress my hair
Tell me always
You'll------be------there.

Filton Hebbard

I'D MAKE YOU MY HONEY

If you were a flower
    and if I were a bee
There'd be nothing in this world
    that we couldn't see
You'd look to the heavens
    for sunshine and rain
Then I'd make you my honey
    and I'd come back again

If you were my honey
    I'd turn myself to bread
And shower you with fancy words
    that I had somewhere read
I'd take all your pollen
    with kisses ever true
And I'd save all my loving
    for no-one else but you

If you were my vision
    and I couldn't see
One touch of your hand, darling
    would light the world for me
I'd see right through the darkness
    the shadows of my life
I'd dress you up in kindness
    and take you as my wife

If you were my lover
    I'd love you all the day
I'd love you through the night-time
    what more could I then say
I'd treat you oh so gently
    give you everything
For you would be the flower
    that's taken all my sting

And if you could see happiness
    in all the things I say
Please find a way to tell me
    and know you've made my day
I'll give you all my worldly wealth
    and share with you my dreams
For you're the one I've longed for
    my love has burst it seams.

Filton Hebbard

I'M NOBODY

I'm so clever
I'm at school
I've stopped learning
I'm a fool
I'm nobody

I don't talk
I sing songs
I've no shoes
I wear thongs
I'm nobody

I don't work
I just play
I've no job
I've no pay
I'm nobody

I don't beg
I've no need
I have bread
I've no greed
I'm nobody

I have love
I am true
I have arms
I hold you
I'm somebody

Yes, I'm somebody
.... truly somebody
Because I have you.

I'VE DREAMT IT MANY TIMES

I've dreamt it once
I've dreamt it twice
I've dreamt it many times
I've dreamt in verse
I've dreamt in song
I've dreamt in nursery rhymes
And every time no matter where
I find you in my arms
I touch your hair and kiss your lips
And take in all your charms
I used to dream of crazy things
Like riding on the moon
Or painting stars upon the sky
With a witches funny broom
But now I only dream of you
Through every night and day
And wish I had the courage to
Just take your hand and say
I'll love you every morning
I'll love you every night
Please let me place my arms around
And hold you oh so tight
I promise I'll stop dreaming
My touch will be quite real
And only with my tenderness
These gentle hands you'll feel
--------------- my love for you
That's bursting at its seams
And wishing for the chance to say
Goodbye to endless dreams
So darling please be kind to me
And linger just a while
I only seek the simple chance
To let you judge my style
Because
My love
You are
It seems
The answer to my world of dreams.

I'VE GOT THAT OLD FEELING

I've got that old feeling again
I thought it had left me but then
You came along
I know I'd been wrong
I've got that old feeling again

My poor heart was jumping with joy
I felt like a kid with a toy
I took hold of your hand
The feeling was grand
I've got that old feeling again

I walked down the street like a prince
I hadn't felt that way dear since
My hair had turned gray
The nights were all day
I've got that old feeling again

I looked at your face and I knew
That only one love wasn't true
For each girl and each boy
have a life to enjoy
I've got that old feeling again

That born again, live again, kiss again,
love again – old, old feeling again.

I THINK OF YOU OFTEN

I think of you often, I think of you now
Is there a limit to what they allow

I long for tomorrow, as I longed for today
To turn on my pillow, my sweetheart and say

You mean so much, darling, your presence like wine
Warms all my emotions, and excites my refine

I need you each moment, each minute, each hour
Just like a garden needs sunshine to flower

I kiss your soft cheek, as my hands touch your hair
My thoughts are the kindest, so now may I dare

With arms that are gentle, embrace you so tight
And stroke you so fondly throughout the night

What kind of a blind fool, is someone like me
For I am the odd one, whom you scarcely see

Whenever you pass by with your fleeting smile
I feel like a stranger, last season's old style

So what must I do now, to earn your sweet love
I've even asked heaven, the Lord up above

To tell me a manner, of how, when or why
For without you beside me, I'd much rather die

So where is the justice, my thoughts do recall
They say is around us, for one and for all

I don't want to wither, on a Summer-dried vine
Like grapes out of season, bypassed for good wine

Until you look my way, one day I do trust
And pass me a welcome, please make it a must

Filton Hebbard

I'll lie with my longing, on my lonely bed
Wishing that my pillow, was you darling, instead

Then I'd turn oh so gently, to kiss you goodnight
And laugh at the pillow..., that I now hug so tight.

JACK AND JILL

If Jack and Jill
went up the hill
to fetch a pail
of water

Perhaps it was Jill
who told the dill
that girls are
someone's daughter

For Jack not Jill
came down the hill
with crown all broke
you see

Whilst I think Jill
allowed a thrill
by showing part
her knee

But Jack not Jill
went further still
and sought what he
was after

And that girl Jill
against her will
said babies are
not laughter.

Filton Hebbard

JENNY LEE

Now I'm down the park
And it's getting dark
And I'm a worried man

Because a girl I know
Said don't you go
I'll catch if I can

Now it isn't long
Since I sang a song
About a girl named Jenny Lee

She was the only one
Who didn't run
When you touched her on the knee

And the scoreboard shook
In the little nook
Of that girl with the brazen ways

But as she grew old
There's a story told
That Jenny caused a craze

For the boys don't chase
They have lost the race
And the girls are hunters now

If you get away
To another day
You simply don't know how

So I'm a worried man
I've got no plan
And I'm cornered in the dark

But if Jenny Lee
Could look and see
She'd think it quite a lark

So what's become
Of the good old mum
Who made the scones and tea

Were they all pure
Dressed in lace demure
But with hearts like Jenny Lee.

Filton Hebbard

JUST TO BE NEAR YOU

Just to be near you
     is heaven to me
Even to see you
     is my ecstasy

To take your soft fingers
     in my roughened hand
Puts me in a kingdom
     the lord of the land

Walking beside you
     is thrill to extreme
Your face is your future
     all peaches and cream

Kissing your sweet lips
     makes my heart a fool
It beats like a learner
     in a lover's first school

But holding you, sweetheart
     so warm and so tight
Is a dream I keep sharing
     with the still of the night.

KISS ME AGAIN

Kiss me again in the morning
    the way that we kissed in the night
Kiss me again in the morning
    then I'll know that everything's right

Hold me so close when it's over
    with thrills running all down my spine
Hold me so close when it's over
    then I'll know that you dear, are mine

Give me your heart like you promised
    with all of the things that we do
Give me your heart like you promised
    then I'll know that our love is true

Touch me my darling so gently
    let me feel warmth in your hand
Touch me my darling so gently
    then I'll know a life ever grand

Pass me your thoughts very softly
    whisper them into my ears
Pass me your thoughts very softly
    then my life will be without fears

Place that gold band on my finger
    with the feeling of words that you say
Place that gold band on my finger
    then I'll know our love will not stray

Kiss me again in the morning
    the way that we kissed in the night
Kiss me again in the morning
    then I'll know that everything's right.

LET ME –I

Let me take you in my arms
    and banish your alarms
        please do

Let me hold you oh so tight
    through each day and darkest night
        please do

Let me stroll with you together
    through rain or sunny weather
        please do

Let me lift you ever high
    like a rainbow in the sky
        please do

Let me tell you from the start
    it's to you I give my heart
        please do

Let me kiss your lips so sweet
    full of loving when we meet
        please do

Let us share a picket fence
    when a family we commence
        please do – please do – please do.

LET ME - II

Let me walk my life beside you
   and hold your tender hand

Let me make all of your dreaming
   and caress in lovers' land

Let me kiss those pretty lips of yours
   and stroke your shiny hair

Let me turn upon my pillow
   and know that you'll be there

Let me grow a field of flowers
   and say they're all for you

Let me tell of my loving
   and my feelings that are true

Let me climb the highest mountain
   and bask the world in song

Let me tell you it's my kingdom
   and that's where you belong

Let me say that I'm not dreaming
   and I'll kiss you as we lie

Let me see your face a-smiling
   and I'll love you till I die.

LIFE

More should be made of the childhood years
When your heart runs free and you have no fears
Of the world that is up ahead

And the thought that your life might be dressed in pain
From the clouds of a future soaked in rain
To you, is for those who are dead

You kick a football with abundant zest
And run like the wind to be as fast as the rest
To your goal that is two shiny posts

And your mind as you trek to your home after school
Is controlled by your stomach most times as a rule
With your thoughts of Mum's puddings and roasts

But the trouble to find and hold work like your Dad
And provide for a family that you've never had
Is a thought that is always alone

For when it arrives with its shattering dreams
And your fingers are grasping at loose ends it seems
To the mercy of fate you are prone

So the pleasures of youth should be cultured some more
And much smaller things should be treasured in store
To be used as relief from the ache

Of sitting alone with your pencil and pad
And seeking paid work from a newspaper ad
That was destined for you to uptake

For it comes as a blow to be out in the world
Where the greed and the schemes of mankind are unfurled
And the ball does not roll at your feet

And the person you loved and kept you so clean
Has taken that journey where she can't be seen
And the mirror reflects nothing sweet

The mirror of course is not screwed to the wall
In a manner so tight that it never will fall
It is hidden quite deep in your mind

And no matter how hard you try to uncover
That wonderful world of your wonderful mother
It is gone – lost forever – so unkind.

Filton Hebbard

LIFE AND LOVING

I don't want to laugh
I don't want to cry
I just want to sing
A sweet lullaby

She said she'd be mine
That girl of my dreams
My heart is not aching
It's bursting its seams

I've taken up dancing
It's all in my head
I had my first lesson
When to me she said

I'll love you my darling
I'll be a true wife
I'll comfort your wishes
For the rest of my life

I'll give you a family
You'll make me a home
My childhood is over
No more will I roam

A son for you, sweetheart
A daughter for me
A wonderful future
That's what I see

So hold me, please tightly
Secure in your arms
No bells will be ringing
We'll have no alarms

For if you're sincere, dear
As I am with you
The things that we've dreamed of
Are about to come true.

LOOKING INWARDS

Let's think about the suffering that happens on this earth
Although it's clad with humans, humanity has dearth

From early days of childhood, we fight amongst each other
The only friend we think we have is the one we know as Mother

We squabble and we argue, we push and shove at school
And relish every chance we get to hand out ridicule

We talk about our neighbour as if we're blemish free
And often thinking at that time of his wife's shapely knee

Should war clouds fall upon us we quickly take up arms
And joyfully make slaughter without the slightest qualms

We have but mild compassion for the old man by the road
He should have made provision, when age became a load

But we treat ever kindly the dog outside our door
And if we think he's hungry, eat up and have some more

We classify that family dog as a creature loyal and fine
He'll rush to bite our enemies yet never drink our wine

But those with whom we fraternize and call our fellow man
We treat with strong suspicion since the day that life began

So maybe it is really true that we the human race
Just yesterday were animals who learned veneer and grace.

Filton Hebbard

LOST LOVES

I was looking through my memories
    and thinking of old friends
The friends I'd lost in anger
    and how could I make amends
I thought of Charles and Harry
    then I thought of Joan and Sue
But my heart turned sentimental
    when my memory filled with you
We were walking through a garden
    on a lovely sunny day
When we stopped to watch the children
    as laughter joined their play
We glanced into each others eyes
    and the emotion in us grew
For we had planned a family
    with a love that we thought was true
But the crazy little quarrels
    that had torn our love apart
Were as foolish as a monkey
    and they cut right through my heart
Now I wonder just how many loves
    are made and lost that way
From the simple lack of courage
    to lift the phone and say
I'm sorry, forgive me please.

LOVE

Take hold of that moment

Don't let it fade

Heaven might vanish

Before it is made

Passion is fleeting

It comes then it goes

Stretch high just to reach it

On the tips of your toes

No need to say pardon

Silence is gold

Romance would be nothing

Without lovers bold

So if you have feeling

To reach up above

Don't let it escape you

That feeling is love.

LOVES AFTERMATH

I cannot take you in dear lass
The old man shook his head
You're too much like your mother
Who's gone to join the dead

You've got the pretty face and form
That she had at your age
I was the one to win her
She was the village rage

We used to go out walking
All round the common square
And I was very proud of her
My heart had not a care

But then her eyes were roaming
O'er friendly hill and dale
And some things kept on telling
That both of us would fail

For even when your father came
And stole her swift away
I knew that she'd return to me
If I could wait the day

It wasn't that I didn't feel
She'd make the finest mother
I think we both knew somehow
That each was for the other

And now you've come to tell me
She gave you my address
Is that the kind of checkmate
In this living game of chess

You say she often spoke of me
With very tender mind
Though not once in my mail box
Did I a letter find

Though I didn't want her writing
Whilst you your father had
For when he died in action
I was so very sad

But after that I waited
Through many long, long years
And though mans' eyes can't do it
My heart shed many tears

I sought no other marriage
So foolish was my plight
I simply walked in solitude
Through every lonely night

It grieves me that she's left us
I hope she's safe above
She was the finest woman
I gave her truest love

But though she didn't correspond
When it was in her power
She sort of willed you on me
And old man and a flower

Perhaps you think I'm brutal
Not what you thought I'd be
But understand please pretty lass
My years of misery

If I had half my living
I'd hug you to my chest
I'd never let you pass me by
The whole world be my test

But then he paused and noticed
The tears well in her eyes
And he knew that his anger
Was heartache dressed in lies

His voice choked as he murmured
Her hand now in his clasp
I always was a foolish man
Good things slip through my grasp

Your mother was the closest
When I was thirty one
But though her eyes were roaming
'Twas I who sought the fun

She would have given marriage
If I had set the date
And though I loved her dearly
Your father made my fate

He took your mother from me
When she was rightly mine
For I sought only gaiety
And samples of sweet wine

I'm glad she sent you to me
My home is yours to keep
I'll leave you my possessions
When comes eternal sleep

I'll treat you as a daughter
My very, very own
Your fragrance is your mothers
Sent back to me on loan

But as she took his offered arm
To stroll the garden path
She knew she was his daughter
Lost love in aftermath.

MAN

Should I sit in a crowd
    or stand in a queue
Or alone on a hill-top
    admiring the view

My mind keeps recalling
    the passages of Man
As he moves through the history
    of when life began

Sometimes he is good
    and sometimes he is bad
Sometimes he is happy
    but often quite sad

He takes from the earth
    the all of its wealth
Quite open and brazen
    without sign of stealth

He seems to ignore
    the rush of the tide
The tide of humanity
    on which we all ride

But one day thank heavens
    I won't be around
When Man tells the world
    he has emptied the ground

And just like the dinosaur
    blundering and strong
He'll wither and die
    but not with a song.

MARYVONNE AND THE HERO OF WATERLOO

She said she'd like to see The Rocks
That reeked Old Sydney Town
The place where history was rich
When razor gangs wore crown

We looked at many houses
From days of yesteryear
All standing like lost soldiers
With vintage not quite clear

She photographed that early church
When garrison ruled hard
Then traversed down the Argyle cut
Hand-made, with walls mock-barred

We wandered through a warehouse
Rough-hewn from ancient tree
Though festooned now with kiosks
That fleeced the world and thee

She indicated with good taste
This lass, from native France
That the Lowenbrau had welcomed
And the sun said here's your chance

We shared three pots of German beer
Maryvonne, my wife and I
So crystal, light and sparkling
Like a brilliant summer sky

She said let's look at Cadman's
The house across the street
Recorded in our history
As the oldest since the Fleet

We then strolled slowly upwards
On an ancient winding road
Dark-dressed both sides with buildings
All weary with time's load

She photographed when at the top
Some other homes refreshed
By paint and legal binding
That the National Trust enmeshed

We then walked to the oldest pub
That one might ever view
Shaped like an angled piece of cake
The Hero of Waterloo

She hesitated at the thought
Of drinking beer within
The sounds were mildly raucous
And the passageways so thin

We sort of bolstered up faint heart
And thrust into the bar
But from that moment onwards
No happenings did mar

She saw within that little pub
The salt of working class
They looked as tough as shearers
And as earthy as wild grass

She looked with some bewilderment
At the three-piece rhythm band
Their castle was their music
And it flowed like running sand

We didn't comment very much
Just stood and took it in
Australia has a roughened base
But we were 'neath the skin

She recollected that fair life
Was three score years and ten
But those musicians numbered three
Had notched that Lord knows when

We watched the violinist play
A lass of Dickens mould
From ruffled blouse to baby shoes
No way would she grow old

She then did share a minor treat
Dear Maryvonne and we
For the pianist called for singers
And from the crowd came he

We saw him put his beer down
Then climb up on the ledge
The smart brown hat upon his head
More firmly he did wedge

She saw him brief the pianist
Like – follow if you can
And with great poise and confidence
Most surely he began

We listened with true courtesy
As his tenor voice rolled out
Then silence grew between us
For this singer was no lout

She made some quiet comment
That the opera was his cue
Though we born of that beaten track
Saw Aussie thru and thru

We thought he might have studied
Or had gift of natural voice
But being of this sunburnt land
Made that small pub his choice

She then did sanction leaving
And we shuffled through the crowd
To breathe the air of evening
Where past convicts cried out loud

We next drove slowly homeward
Reflecting on that scene
In the hotel that was Waterloo
To less Hero than has-been

But that little taste of Sydney
In the rocks up on the hill
I'm sure must live with Maryvonne
As the old Australian will.

Filton Hebbard

MENTAL FATALITY

I watch the eventide pass by
    as in the mirror of my mind I lie

I see the things I never saw
    when I was coasting evermore

Those childhood years seemed far away
    yet reflected back like yesterday

And clear as ink I know I yearned
    for knowledge that I never learned

I saw my life from early years
    and my mind floated in my tears

As all the things I planned to do
    weren't half as clear as Irish stew

I'd wasted so much of my time
    on tunes that lacked a decent rhyme

I'd though tomorrow soon enough
    to start the elementary stuff

But now within my senior age
    tomorrow soon I won't engage

For though my mind will never rust
    it'll help to form cremation dust

And all those wondrous things to do
    so sadly I must leave to you.

MENTAL REVENGE

He was a pleasant little man
His wife was somewhat large
Whenever they decisions made
The lady did take charge

She pushed him out the door each morn
And let him in each night
Her upraised hand to touch her hair
Caused him to cringe in fright

She made him wash the dishes
And sometimes scrub the floor
She dressed in modern finery
Though he looked rather poor

She walked two paces in the front
Whenever they were out
He couldn't keep the speed up
Not with his twinge of gout

He'd start the paper crossword
His pleasures were quite thin
And she would take it from him
To wrap the garbage in

Sometimes when she had feeling
For the sweetest nuptial joy
She'd lift him to position
As if he were a toy

Now this poor chap did sicken
He'd had one day enough
Though he did hide his feelings
Least she his ear did cuff

He hadn't planned their marriage
He then did recollect
'Twas she who'd made proposal
With he, alas, henpecked

But even if a little man
Can't fend himself too well
At least his wishful thinking
Put his old girl in hell

He got one day amusing
On quite a devilish scheme
To let him see her naked
She'd never ever dream

With her great love of eating
She weighed at sixteen stone
Whilst with the life she gave him
He was just skin and bone

She often told him proudly
That she'd been virgin pure
A huge, though white-draped lady
To the alter he did lure

And it did always puzzle him
Why she did not rejoice
Some virgins were from self-respect
The others had no choice

And also as you might suspect
This man had hairless head
Which after they made love at night
His bumps she often read

They holidayed each summer
At a motel rather swank
Where the casual staff were beatnik
The men's hair thick and lank

So this wee man did buy a wig
And hid it safe away
He knew his wife would ask of him
Most times on Saturday

Well on this great historic night
Whilst she hid form in dark
Our little man was given chance
To follow through his lark

He sneaked off to the bathroom
A normal thing to do
And stuck his wig upon his head
With a quick-grip kind of glue

And chuckling deep inside himself
The best part of it all
He did what she demanded
And let pyjamas fall

So later when she reached for him
To knead his head like dough
She stiffened with paralysis
Oh what a ghastly blow

And as she was recovering
From this romantic sin
He'd done the near impossible
At least he'd had a win

He got from out the covers
And raced straight through the door
To scoop as he did rush away
His clothes from off the floor

Now even though that secret
To no-one did he tell
The change was quite miraculous
In his wife Two-Ton Nell.

MINERS WIVES

Their skins were like parchment
Thick dust in their hair
Their hearts knew the rent
Of a woman's despair
When a man sees no reason
Why they raise a mind
To the heat that's in season
And relief they can't find

Though love has strong wings
In a marriage of bliss
The bondage it brings
Doesn't hinge on a kiss
For if man takes a girl
And uses her youth
Her heart's in a whirl
Till she learns the truth

For a rough mining town
Is a curse of a place
Where thirsts always drown
At expense of fine lace
And when man oh so often
His wife does behold
As a vent to his passion
Before she grows old

And his wife all this while
Simply withers away
With clothes out of style
And the heat of the day
For if a man doesn't offer
His money to spend
How can his wife proffer
The joys of days end

Those wings might take hold
Those founded on love
But if he's not careful
The flight won't be dove
For gone is the time
Of the old rocking chair
Where a woman made rhyme
With a shawl round her hair

It's quite bad enough
To tolerate weather
When you're big, strong and tough
With a skin coarse as leather
But a woman deep under
Is soft, sweet and kind
Don't tear her asunder
If she is refined

Give love and affection
You great, mining brute
There's time for correction
And share of the loot
A woman is willing
For all of her years
She yearns for a thrilling
Not sun-dried-out tears.

MY GIRL IS A HONEY

Now, my girl is a honey
The sweetness of my life
You'll never know the feeling
When she said she'd be my wife
I put my arms around her
And held her oh so tight
She said she would be true to me
I was her Mister Right
I walk the street beside her
And smile at everyone
My happiness I want to share
I've put blues on the run
And I must say to all the world
It's loving you must find
To drive away your troubles
And thoughts that are unkind
But if you need a reason
To see what love can do
Just come and meet my honey
She'll put a spell on you
With a smile that came from heaven
As sweet as from the bee
And then you'll know the reason
For what love's done to me.

MY HEAD CALLED ME A CLOWN

I cared not for the thunder
    nor the rain that tumbled down
My heart called me romantic
    and my head called me a clown
I couldn't see a reason
    why love should pass me by
While I had the strength to grasp it
    and with it sometimes lie
The thunder rattled windows
    and the rain soaked into me
But I stood on the corner
    for a special girl to see
I think I looked ridiculous
    as sometimes lovers do
But my heart was romantic
    and I agreed it's true
And when my girl, she waved to me
    from a shiny limousine
She was as dry as tinder
    and I felt somewhat green
For the driver grinned derisive
    and my girl turned her thumbs down
And my tail stopped its wagging
    when my head called me a clown
Now I wander homewards
    I sing a little song
It's all about life's lessons
    that teach us right from wrong
For getting caught together
    when the rain comes tumbling down
Two hearts might call romantic
    if they should almost drown
But waiting in a rainstorm
    as romantic as could be
Is not impassioned loving
    as any girl could see
Now I cared not for thunder
    nor the rain that tumbled down

But my heart called me romantic
    and my head called me a clown.

MY HEART YOU'LL ALWAYS OWN

I cannot think of life without you
Was I alive before
You played upon my heart strings
Turned the key in that locked door
I had always thought that loving
Was a story book gazette
But why was I so foolish
When true love I'd never met
But now that I have found you
I understand the pain
Of the ones whose hearts are broken
Saying they'd not love again
For that is how I feel dear
I cannot get you from my mind
You are there throughout the daytime
In my dreams I do you find
I am like a wounded soldier
Or a puppet on a string
I will answer to your wishes
Name a tune and I will sing
For darling please believe me
You are the only one
Who could ever share my heaven
And turn cloudy days to sun
But I will make a promise
To you and you alone
That no matter what might happen
My heart you'll always own.

THE LUCKIEST GIRL

Forgiving is understanding, but understanding is not always forgiving.
Sometimes we need to share troubles before we choose a path.

The sea was violent. He had seen the signs and knew that he should have headed back to shore an hour earlier; but he hadn't, he'd taken the risk and he had not regretted it.

He was a fisherman, an old hand at the game. He'd been a fisherman since childhood, and now, at over sixty years of age, he was still a fisherman; a tired fisherman.

The signs had been clear and he'd ignored them. That dark line creeping out of the horizon should have been signal enough, but the catch had been poor that day so he'd stayed longer. Damn fool! No, lucky fool, maybe.

But he'd been a fool all his life, hadn't he? Life was for the young, for fun, wasn't it? Spending all of his free time in the bar with his mates; fondling the girls; buying them things and getting favours in return. Well........... until pregnancy. Who invented pregnancy? Girls knew how to look after themselves, didn't they? Wasn't that the way it was supposed to go? Emancipation; freedom of spirit and all that. Girls could seek what they wanted now; no need to bottle it up. They could be their own boss so far as sex was concerned, couldn't they?

Nearly fifty years of age he'd been, when the announcement was made. "I'm pregnant".

Hell. Had that been a turning point!! More of a shock than anything else. And from a girl who hadn't been anything special at the time.

Good God, he'd better stop reminiscing. He furled the sail of his little boat to let it wash with the sea. That was all he could do. He couldn't fight the sea. Hardly fifteen feet in length, open in the middle, a locker in the prow and a couple of boxed thwarts at the back (more for buoyancy than anything else .... if the need arose).

A killer wave had crashed into the gunwale of the boat and thrown him sidewards. One of those rotten waves that, for reasons of their own, seemed to suddenly rear up to break the uniformity of size, then make a laughing sound as they tried to drag all things smaller into their rolling depths.

Instinctively, he grasped the mast as the wave hit, and his knuckles showed white through his brown weathered skin. For a moment, he looked at them. Was it the white of tension and physical strain, or was it the desperate whiteness of fear?

He had no fear for himself. A man had to be a man. He had chosen a way of life, or life had chosen a way of living for him. But he did care about his little girl, his daughter, the only thing that mattered now.

Twelve years of age she was; pretty too. And so wonderfully affectionate. "Look, Papa," she'd say, "I made this for you". How many times had she said that throughout the years? Maybe fifty times. And what had he done with the treasures she'd made. He'd pinned them to the walls of his room.

113

He didn't share a bed with his wife these days; and he did his best to forget the reason why. Was it sad or was it silly; or had fate intervened? Fate seemed nearer the mark................, the way the cookie crumbled in life.

And what had his daughter 'made' that he'd pinned to the walls of his room? A sketch, a drawing, or a water colour painting. Actually, 'made' wasn't quite the right description, but they were from his girl and he'd retained them – a personal gallery of love.

"What have you made for me today, sweetheart," he'd say, as she'd come towards him with a smile on her face and a sheet of paper waving in one hand.

"Guess, Papa," she'd say.

"A fish, a crab, a bird, a dog"?

Each time she'd shake her head, her smile growing wider. Then she'd show it to him. It would be a sketch of himself.

"Beautiful," he'd say. "You make me more handsome every time".

Then she'd bury her face into the waist of his shirt and he knew that there would be tears welling in her eyes just as there were in his own.

He never asked her why she didn't draw her mother. Maybe she did and her mother pinned them to the walls of her room, too. Her special room that he never entered.

But the early childlike, if loving, attempts to draw him had slowly been replaced by portraits of increasing quality. And he saw in them a future for his girl; a future that he'd never seen, or been encouraged to see, for himself; a future greater than the sight of fish twitching in a basket at his feet.

The white of his knuckles was gradually turning back to gnarled brown, and he grasped the baler, its security cord now twisted around his water-filled boots, and anxiously began scooping the excess water from his boat.

The sky had darkened even more, he noticed, and an ensuing storm was a certainty. But the risk of staying beyond the time of commonsense and safety had been worthwhile, or so he now thought. Two huge fish, wrapped in a piece of worn, discarded sail, were tucked firmly beneath a straight thwart towards the prow of his boat.

They would make his daughter smile, and the pleasure he'd feel at this would make the pain, fear and hardship vanish. Perhaps he'd say, "Maybe you would make one for me, sweetheart." And she would smile and say "Yes, Papa. I will make one for you." But when she handed it to him, he knew that it would be another drawing of himself, and he'd say, "It's lovely – I will pin it on the wall with the others."

The boat swayed beneath him and he shoved at the tiller to help it back to where it ran with the sea, not against it. The wall of black sky was almost overhead now and ahead of him, land was not yet in sight. He'd been through these situations before and taken them in his stride, so to speak, but those thoughts about his daughter kept returning unbidden. She'd be at school. No, he glanced at his watch, on her way home most likely. Or talking to her friends maybe.

She liked to talk. Not silly talk though. "Old for her age", his own friends had said to him occasionally – "got sense, must have got it from you, Paulo."

He never replied to that type of talk. What should a man do when half the village knew that he'd been caught out – marrying simply because he believed it was the proper thing to do. How could a man dump a pregnant girl when he'd had sex with her about half a dozen times. In the cities, there was always someone who knew a 'shonky' doctor who could 'fix it up'; but not in this little village, with eyes behind every window. You'd need a heart like a lion to have the courage to knock on the door of a 'clinic'.

Such a good-looker that wife of his. "Nymphomaniac", someone had said, and he hadn't bothered to answer because he hadn't cared at the time. They weren't married then, just casual bed-mates............... and there hadn't been anything abnormal about her behaviour.

But if he heard any insulting references to her now, that person would be swallowing a few of his own front teeth.

So why did she have a special bedroom of her own? He'd built it for her and never shared it with her, not even once. Life could sure turn rotten sometimes.

Nymphomania. Such an easy word to misinterpret. How wrong people could be. She wasn't like that at all. Not really. Just the way life played its tricks on people. The street a person walked depended on whether you were rich or poor.

Bur brother! How that baby had changed his life. He was a father. It was a marvellous feeling. The little smile beaming up at him from out of the cot was worth an ocean of fish.

God damn it, he'd have to be careful! He nearly went over the side that time as a wall of water washed over him. And it was just as well the baler was on a tether or he'd be panicking about the amount of water swilling around his ankles; inside the boat, not outside where it belonged.

He recommended scooping it out, a tide of desperation rising within him. Was he panicking? Was his intuition telling him that this storm would be worse than any he'd outlived before, that he might not make it home this time?

What would his little girl do if he failed to return? Only twelve years of age – she seemed not much older than the baby she'd been a couple of years before.

Another wave spilt over the gunwale as the boat spun sidewards across the run of the water. He tugged at the rope that controlled the tiller when he sat amidships to give the boat better trim, and his heart leapt as the rope in his left hand felt loose. The rope tightened again – thank God for that. It had only been the way the water swirled – another of its nasty tricks.

The excess water taken in was now adding to his plight; making the boat move sluggishly and impeding its buoyancy. Smaller waves were now breaking into the boat and he knew he would have to move quickly to get the water out or it might wallow and go under. He lashed the tiller rope to the mast and baled frantically at the water now engulfing his boots.

Suddenly, there was a lull in the savagery of the sea; as if it had forgotten its temper and decided to lay quiet for a while. He took full advantage of it and was thankful for the chance to get most of the water out of the bilges and back into the sea where it belonged.

Splashes of rain hit his cheeks. The sky was completely dark and an ominous grey mist that hovered over the water did little to help his uneasiness. Where on earth was he? He could be anywhere – there was still no land in sight. Had it all sunk? He hadn't been out all that far, had he? How far out had those fish pulled him before he managed to drag them aboard? He'd been trailing a multiple line when they'd struck simultaneously, both of them tugging the lines like tethered dogs gone berserk at the sight of the neighbour's cat.

Had he been standing at the time, he'd have been jettisoned overboard. But he wouldn't have been standing. Too old in the head for that; with fishing anyhow.

When had he first started to fish for a living? Hell. He drew the waterproof headpiece that dangled at the back of his neck over his thick gray hair. A sudden squall thrashed the little boat with heavy rain, then passed on.

When had he first started to fish for a living after his father had been killed in that stupid war? How old had he been? Twelve years of age. His daughter's age. And there he was still thinking of her as a baby.

He laughed; not with humour, but at his own stupidity.

What did he know at twelve years of age that he wasn't supposed to know about until he was older? Not much about fishing, but damn near everything about 'the birds and the bees', as adults put it.

Did his daughter know those things?

It wasn't the rain that soaked him now. Perspiration poured out of him. What had her mother been saying to the girl whilst he'd been out fishing?

Hell no, not that. Not that mother-like daughter, or daughter-like-mother stuff.

He eased into self-assurance. That girl of his was too much like Papa, too much of a thinker.

He recalled the first time he'd hooked his thumb over her waistband elastic, long before their marriage. She'd held his hand, that pretty wife of his, and that soft smile had run across her lips. "I have to eat, Paulo," she'd said.

He'd hesitated, "How much?"

She'd mentioned a sum; not enough really, but he'd willingly paid. When a man wasn't married he had to fish around for certain things that cured a pain; and he didn't mean with a fishing line.

But how did she live on that skimpy amount? He guessed she asked the same from all of the others until one of his drinking mates set him straight.

"The village bike won't let anybody else touch her now, Paulo – only you. It looks like you've won the race."

There'd been a flush of ego until he thought about it. How could she manage to eat on the small amount she asked of him? And there were times she refused to take anything.

"I did a couple of days work in the little hospital, Paulo. It was enough. I just want to be with you."

That had sounded good before the pregnancy. He'd thought he'd never marry – just keep jogging along like an old horse.

Funny how a fixed opinion could change – you think a certain way about a thing; then, suddenly, something happens to throw a different light altogether on it. Makes you feel foolish.

Take marriage for example.

A priest, or a parson or some other governmental freak says a few words and tells a man and a woman that they can sleep together and the neighbours clap hands. Perhaps they all do a little dance, have some wine and eat a bit of cake.

But a girl who can't afford the cake and satisfies with bread, is a rubbish bin.

The world sure has some rotten edges. Well, the world itself was sound enough; but society, the people in it, who taught them to draw the line on right or wrong?

A man gets a pain in his chest and he hurries to a doctor. The doctor listens to a recounting of the pain, makes a decision, prescribes an appropriate medicine, charges a handsome fee, and the man is both pleased and humble. The doctor is marvellous.

Another man gets a different type of pain, hurries to a woman he knows for a suitable treatment, she provides the appropriate medicine, charges a fee (a good deal less than the doctor's), and that man is pleased and joyful.

The woman, however, is treated like a tramp.

Why? Because she took money for her cure.................. just like the doctor.

'One girl can hand out more medicine than half a dozen quacks', he'd heard a friend of his father say on one occasion. There'd been a grin, and laugh to go with it.

And what had his father replied. "Yeah." One word, uttered unhesitatingly, had covered it.

A 'quack' was a doctor of course. Not a very respectful way to put it, but understood just the same.

Was one cure necessarily any better than the other? Each man had gone to a doctor of his choice, paid his money, and taken his 'medicine'.

Why was sex the source of so much gossip? The world would be a very empty place without it.

A wave bucked the boat and he steadied himself. But his reflections returned.

Everybody was so damned poor in a fishing village. Unless you were a 'big-time fisherman', with a vessel that could stay out for a week or more if needs be; in a boat that really looked like a boat.

So why was he a fisherman? Because his mother was suddenly on her own, with a solid home, a twelve year old son, and no money.

And to a boy, fishing was fun. What a wonderful way to make a living – having fun.

He grinned.

Then he criticised himself. Nobody made a decent living having fun. When did a man wake up? Did he have to be thinking about the price of a 'box' before he realised that life was nearly over? A burial box of course; a coffin.

But he had been fortunate, in a particular way; his father had been a builder. Yes, not only a builder of small cottages, but a builder of the mind.

Strange how things seemed to pass down in family ties; the same skills, the same appreciation of words, the same thoughts about right and wrong.

It was a religion of its own making; family religion, with a god of its own, the god of knowledge. "This country is at war, Paulo," his father had said to him one Sunday morning as they had both stood watching from the elevated position of their home. They'd been watching the small crowd swelling before the church doors, a scene that they had silently shared; a nice scene, in its own manner, one of orderliness and respect.

Men and women in their better finery, freshly bathed, hair combed, and conscious of their duty to suppress vulgarity, at least until the service was over.

Paulo's parents did not attend church. "It is a fool's paradise," Paulo's father said on one occasion. "Think, son. There is no need for it. If you want to say 'thank you' for anything, you don't have to go to special building to say it. And think of the pain and suffering we experience. Do we have to offer thanks for that?"

But it was not his father's thoughts on accredited religion that came to Paulo's mind at that moment; it was the few words that had been offered about the war, all those many years ago.

"I am going to join the Army as a duty, Paulo, and if I don't return, you must take care of your mother. She has a strong mind but she is not strong in the body. You are lucky that way. It is in the mind where we need strength, not in the arms and legs. Those parts, the physical parts, they might have the power to carry heavy weights, but the mind has no muscles, yet is the most powerful part of us."

"You know I have many books. You must read them all. You must read them again – and again and again, if necessary, until you know what the writer meant when he chose those words. He was passing his knowledge to the reader, building a mind from a hill to mountain."

As those thoughts and recollections returned to him, Paulo pondered over his own misbehaviour; his own lack of appreciation of his father's words.

As a boy, had he heeded his father's advice – of course not, he would find his own path.

And where was that path? It did not exist. The sea had no path, no gutters, no footpaths, no guiding lines.

The sea ran into every nook and cranny it could find.

And when did that realisation first fall upon him? Not until he had seen his baby daughter for the first time.

And what he done about it?

With hollow stomach, he had read his father's books. Until then, he had been a fisherman. He had done nothing.

But when his father had not returned from the War, what was that other part of his father's story that had been brushed aside with the growing pains of youth. Well, it had been accompanied with a wave of the hand; a gesture.

"Those people down there, Paulo, believe in a god that's supposed to help us in life. I believe in this new thing they've discovered. They call it genes; something in us that gets passed up the ladder, not down, like they say about other things. It's found in behaviour, natural skills, habits, sense of fairness and humour, all of the things that make a person what he is. That's what they call genes. Don't know how they woke up to it but it makes sense.

But it's not one step after the other like a real ladder, it has missing treads. A sort of lucky dip. You might have your parents good or bad features or habits. Or it could be your grandfathers from either side, or your great-grandparents. No set pattern, but still floating around.

These things that we build into ourselves become part of our minds – the place where we hide all of our real treasures – and it gets passed on, Paulo, just like the big feet or hands or the muscles. Some of it gets locked in, I'm sure of it. When we can think and act like one of our forbears we are releasing a bit of our inheritance, showing it, good or bad, that's what we are doing."

Paulo's palm thumped his own forehead. What was he passing on, good or bad?

Fishing! What a hopeless sort of a way to make a living in a little open boat. A man could do all right sometimes when he landed a couple like those two beauties tucked up under those thwarts as if they owned the boat and everything in it – still giving a bit of a twitch now and then to prove they were still alive.

Christ! That patch of calmer water had been replaced with its wilder, rougher relative. A wave shoved the little boat sidewards and soaked him as it did so.

He commenced baling again, cursing himself. This was no time for daydreaming or reprehending himself for what he had or hadn't done with his life. He peered at his watch again, – 4.35 pm. Well, that had a bit to do with why it was darker. And no land in sight yet.

That little girl of his would be home from school; and worried. Not because of the hour, sometimes he stayed out until sundown; but because of the dark and the horrible weather.

Anyhow, he still had those two fish. She'd be goggle-eyed when she saw those.

"Gee, Papa, they're both bigger than me."

"Yes, sweetheart, and when I sell them, I'm going to buy you that lovely dress we saw in the shop."

"No, Papa, you save the money for when you don't go out fishing any more. I don't like it when I know I can't see you."

"But little girls have to have nice dresses."

"No, Papa, little girls have to have nice papas – like you."

And he'd hug her, and tears they'd both try to hide would fill their eyes.

That's how it would be when he reached the shore. He knew it, simply knew it.

But whose fault would the money shortage be? His own? Of course it would be his own. What had he done for nearly fifty years of his life? Become a fisherman in a little boat – having fun. What sort of a man was he? Did he deserve to have such a lovely daughter depending on him for her future? And a working wife?

That room. His wife's room. He'd built that room, hadn't he? And she'd made it clear why she wanted it.

God! The weather had worsened. The sky had blackened to a cloak of midnight, obscuring all the sparkling celestial sign-posts that would normally have guided a mariner towards home.

The boat was wallowing again, with the water halfway to his knees. Hell, how did that get in there?

Frantically, he baled, and for the first time in his fisherman's life he suffered real fear. He mustn't die; he owed his own life to his daughter, the child he'd created in his 'cure' for sex.

What would she do without him? Fall into the clutches of some other man who was looking for that age-old cure?

No, dammit. He was panicking for nothing. He was a fisherman who'd been out there, by himself, at least ten thousand times. Why should he think this particular day had any special omen in it? Sure, he was in the middle of a storm, but he'd out-ridden lots of storms before; even laughed about them.

Storms came, storms went, the sunshine ruled supreme.

It was great to be out on the water on a sunny day. You could reflect on things; sort of in peace, just drifting along.

You could sing if you wanted to, with nobody around to jeer at your out-of-tune voice.

'Drifting along'. The words came back to him.

That American fellow sang a song about drifting along. A cowboy's song. That Bing Crosby fellow. Sitting on a horse he'd been when they'd recorded it.

"Drifting along with the tumbling tumbleweeds" were the words that came to mind. Something like that.

Silly, really. Imagine sitting on a horse all day watching cows? What a way to make a living. A man would get warts or corns on his arse doing that. He'd have to, surely?

God dammit! Why was he thinking of all these things?

Why now? Well, because he was worried and didn't want to let on to himself that he was worried.

Why? Because her mother was in hospital; a special wing of the hospital. Not that the girl would be in a hurry to get there and visit, but because she would be alone.

"I like talking to you, Papa," she'd said on one occasion. "I learn things."

"And I like to be home with you, sweetheart," he'd replied.

So why was he out there in a little boat, day after day, if he liked to be at home?

He answered himself. Because I'm a fool. He muttered it, half aloud. A bloody fool. I drifted along with those tumbleweeds.

What was a tumbleweed? A weed that dried up in the summer, tangled itself into a ball, and rolled away, a slave to whichever way the wind was blowing.

He looked down at his limbs. Well, he wasn't a weed, he was strong. But the rest of it was near the truth; the tumbling part.

He'd drifted into fishing for a living because it was easy and his mother needed income – but he could have gotten out of it as he'd grown older – and he hadn't.

And when that girl said she was pregnant, he could have gotten out of that too – and he hadn't.

"She's the village bike," came back to him. "Don't waste good dough on flowers and stuff."

And he hadn't. And why hadn't she taken a girl's precaution? He didn't know. Somehow he didn't care. It was another stage of drifting along – a slave to his apathy.

But the child was truly his. Ben had checked the blood group for him.

Ben was the local doctor. They'd spent their early childhood days together.

The kids whose fathers knew him, called him Uncle Ben; a benign, old man with a gentle smile.

He'd conveyed the horrifying news.

"You'd better come in for a check," he'd said. "I hate to be the one to tell you, but that wife of yours is a sick woman."

"How bad, Ben? What is it?"

"Its syphilis, Paulo. Advanced, I'm afraid. A check-up is vital for you."

"Haven't been in the same cot for five years, Ben. What's the treatment?"

"Long and slow here. Weekly arsenic injections. The big cities knock it over quick."

"I see."

"No ulcers, or rash down below?"

"No."

"You know I'll have to ask her who might be infected?"

"Of course, Ben. But don't tell me the numbers." There weren't any smiles in the conversation. Just sickness to the pit of his stomach.

And that news had been yesterday, before he'd hurried to his boat and moved with the tide. It had been rotten news that had given him a sickening guilt. How much of the blame was his own?

He'd left a note for his daughter. "Your mother's sick, sweetheart, wait till I get home."

His mind was jerked back into the present as water rushed over the gunwale, and the boat lurched with the heavy sea. He'd better get out of this mess before he gave thoughts to another.

He baled again, savagely, almost hating the water as he jettisoned it out, out of his life. But his savagery made him careless, and the spar, no longer holding the spread of the sail, spun freely and struck his head, knocking him face-down into the water that lay in the boat. He clutched at the base of the mast and clung to it, by now soaking wet and mentally sick; sick and confused.

Had that whack on his head bought home the reality of his life; the aimless tumbleweed existence of those long years?

He wasn't a fool, he was a mess; a mess that now had to survive and overcome the fact that he suddenly had a depth of responsibility that he had previously only skimmed the surface.

No point in trying to bale now. The water was constantly breaking over the gunwale with every surge of the sea. But it was a wooden boat; and it would float.

In the locker, behind the prow, was a personal buoyancy float. Silly thing really; his daughter had made it for him, two, maybe three years before.

"To keep you safe, Papa," she'd said.

"Thank you, sweetheart, I'll leave it in my boat and think of you every time I put it on."

He'd never worn it, but he'd kept his word and taken it to sea; part of the furniture that was never used.

If he drowned, if he died out there, if he washed away under the pitch, black heaven, he wanted her to know that he was thinking of her – thanking her for caring. So he'd wear it now.

He checked his own tether that shared his waist with the bottom of the mast and crawled towards the locker. The two, huge fish were still tight in their captivity, wriggling more now that they were covered in the water of their birth; wondering, perhaps, why they couldn't move.

He reached the locker; no need to worry about it adding to the buoyancy, the door was not a perfect fit. But he opened it slowly, to reach inside and fumble for his daughter's gift, slowly withdrawing it into sight.

He could have laughed but it was too serious for laughter. He'd tried it on when his daughter had given it to him, and at the time had thought it to be the only time, the time to please a child.

"Perfect fit, sweetheart," he'd said.

It was two empty, four litre plastic bottles, caps screwed tight, with a short, leather strap-like dog's collar threaded through the handles.

"It's to keep your head out of the water, Papa," she'd said with a serious tone, "the buckle is at the front."

Half-crouched at the locker door, he sprawled sidewards as a wave burst over the prow, spinning him back towards the mast.

Floating, partly over one side of the boat, held by his safety tether, he managed to buckle the plastic bottles around his neck, then struggled to establish a position of security.

The sail spar spun again with its limited movement and ferocity of the wind, and he lay senseless in the well of the boat, lifting and swaying with the lurch of the water as the tempest around him continued to moodily play havoc with his craft.

Unconscious, his body moved aimlessly by the surging water. With the tether around his waist and attached to the mast at the other end, he floated. The tether had been long enough to allow him access to all parts of the boat, but out of physical control now, he was sometimes in the sea and sometimes in the boat. But held by the plastic bottles, his head was up, and he was breathing.

He awoke to brilliant sunshine, a cloudless sky, and a flat sea. Night had come and gone. His head ached; ruefully he ran a hand over the sore bumps on the back of his neck, trying to recount the events that had led him to the circumstances in which he lay. For the moment they were vague, but he struggled to a sitting position and took stock of his surroundings. Unsure of himself, he left the two empty bottles that had kept his head above water to remain as they were. As clumsy and primitive as they might appear to some, he knew they had saved him from drowning. Almost laughable, but the truth.

Thank God for wooden boats; to hell with those plastic, streamlined craft flooding the market.

He sized his immediate future.

Before he had been knocked unconscious the boat had been filled to the edge of the gunwale, but now the gunwale was a few inches above the outside level. In several places, immediately beneath the rim, the lower timber had weathered and parted to allow a narrow crack through which the high level of water inside had seeped out to a lower level. With care, if he baled quickly, he could empty enough to prevent its return.

He reached for the rope to pull the baling bucket to him, then gave a spontaneous burst of laughter. He'd forgotten the two large tuna. They were still jammed where he had put them. How lucky could a man be sometimes? Lucky, he thought. Is that what he told himself? Well, lucky enough to have a daughter who wanted him alive.

It took him an hour to empty the boat of its unwanted water. He looked at the time on his waterproof watch, at the location of the sun, felt the mild breeze, unfurled the sail that wrapped around the mast, and sailed for home.

It was late afternoon before he arrived. He'd stripped off and sat naked until the sun and the movement had dried his clothes which he'd tied to the sail ropes.

There was a small crowd waiting to greet him on the beach. Fisher-folk were like that; they were concerned for each other. Small boats didn't stay out all night in that season, even if so in others.

His daughter was there, running to hug him as the keel dragged on the sand. "I worry for you, Papa."

Proudly, he presented the fish. "For you, sweetheart."

She scarcely glanced at the fish, "No, for you when you don't go fishing any more." Tears flooded her eyes.

A friend took care of the fish.

He moored the boat to one of the iron loops that had been imbedded into the concrete wall that retained the wash of higher tides. With an anchor thrust into the sand at the stern it was safe enough in moderate weather.

They walked to their home in silence, an arm around each other's waists, the firmness of their touch taking care of needless speech.

At the cottage door, he held it open with one out-stretched arm as she entered. "I'll bathe," he said. "The salty water has dried on me. Then we'll visit your mother."

During their walk from the shore she had not enquired of her mother's illness and he was conscious of the pause before she replied. "You go, Papa. I will stay here and make dinner."

"Sweetheart, please," he protested. "She will want to see you. Your mother loves you. She buys you nice things whenever she can, and you never cuddle her like you cuddle me. It must hurt her."

Her solemn face looked up at him. "It is hard for me to tell you, Papa."

"Please. Whatever it is you must tell me. You must. We must fix it."

She shook her head.

"Sweetheart, please," he implored. "She gave you life. You never draw her. You have drawn me twenty times; maybe more. Maybe fifty times."

Without further comment, she left him and went to her room. She was gently waving a sheet of artist's paper, her face stoic, as she returned.

To change the conversation and topic, he gave a laugh. "What is it? A house, an elephant, a monkey? No, it is me in my boat."

He was certain that it would be another portrait of himself. But he felt his face tighten as he looked at it.

It was not a drawing of a house, or elephant, or a monkey; not even of him in his boat. It was a drawing of his wife, her mother. Her blond hair flowing across the pillow, her blue eyes shining, a smile on her lips – with her legs drawn up, her knees wide apart – and lying on her was a goat.

He felt his body shake. The scene shocked him and he could not look up.

From behind her back, the child produced a cluster of similar sheets and handed them to him. Then she ran from the room, crying.

Slowly, he looked through them, like the shuffling of a pack of cards; there would have been twenty, maybe thirty. Always, her mother, lying there, smiling, knees up and the nipples of her breasts falling slightly outwards with the looseness of age; and crouched over her, the creatures that he often suggested that the child had drawn – a monkey, a goat, a sheep, and other species he had never seen.

He placed the drawings in his room and walked outside. He knew that he badly needed to bathe, but it could wait. His heart raced.

In the small garden that lay in an enclave that gave access to the special room that his wife had asked him to build, was an outdoor seat; designed to accommodate three or four. His daughter was there, her hands to her face.

He sat beside her, placing his arm around her as she buried her tears into his wrinkled shirt front.

After a while, he spoke. "When did you draw them, sweetheart?"

"When you were fishing and I heard laughing. That little window. I climbed on a box."

He moved his palm gently up and down her upper arm, in a soothing wave. "But why the animals?"

"They looked like animals to me, Papa – the animals you thought I had drawn."

"And you knew what they were doing?"

"Yes."

"How long have you known?"

"The big girls at school talk. A long time, Papa. I'm sorry." Her tears poured out again.

He hesitated. How deep could he take their conversation? She was the same age as he had been when his father had left to participate in a war from which he had not returned. And what had he done with his father's advice and thoughts?

Nothing. Sweet nothing, was the answer to that.

And boys were boys, they were not pretty little girls.

Boys swam naked together in a sheltered recess on the beach. They talked openly about sex and other related things. They made derisive remarks about each others penises.

"Look at Fatty's big dick. Must be a wanker. Are you a wanker, Fatty? How often do you play a tune?"

Twelve year old girls didn't go on like that, surely?

"The big girls at school talk," she'd said. What exactly did they say and how much of it did those big girls make up? The exaggerations, the ego, know-all bit, the skiting.

So easy for his father to talk to him. Sort of man-to-man stuff.

But girls – he didn't know.

Well, he would take it as far as he could – not being a big girl at school.

"And that is why you don't want to visit your mother at the hospital? She has always been kind to you."

She looked up. "But not to you, Papa."

"Your mother gave me you, and you are the most wonderful gift that I have ever received or will be likely to receive again. What would my life be without you?"

She wiped a fresh flood of tears onto his shirt.

"You are young," he said, "far too young for these sorts of things, but my friends say that you have an old head – inside they mean. Do you understand?"

"No, I don't think so. But I always listen to what you say. I always did."

"Will you listen now, if I talk to you as if I know that inside your head you are old, like my friends say - very old, even though I know that you are only twelve?"

"I will try."

"Last night, out on the water, I thought I might drown and never see you again."

She looked up. "I think I knew, Papa. Something told me. I sat on the ledge all night – frightened to leave."

"The ledge where we used to sit and chat when you were little?"

"Yes. Uncle Ben came down to talk to me. He told me Mumma was in hospital. But he didn't say why. He said it was too dark for me to see you even if you did come in at night. He said I should go home to bed. He asked me if I'd had anything to eat."

"Did you do that – go home?"

"No. I said 'thank you, Uncle Ben, and after a while he left."

There was a short silence between them, then she added. "You said you wanted to talk to me like I was older."

"Yes. It isn't easy, sweetheart. Knowing where to start is very hard."

"Start at the beginning, Papa. That is what the teacher says."

"It starts when I was very young – the same age that you are now."

"Good. And while I listen, I'll pretend I am a boy, just like you."

"You mentioned your teacher."

"Yes."

"We are all teachers, sweetheart. We are born to be teachers, even though we might never know it or think of ourselves as teachers."

"Sums and spelling and all that?"

"No. Not that kind of teaching. The teaching of life. What is good to do and say, and what is wrong to do and say. Sometimes we teach ourselves by the things that we do and sometimes others teach us by the things that they do. And there are times when we think we have learnt something and we discover, maybe years later, that it was not correct and what we told others as right, was very wrong."

Dry-eyed now, she looked up. "What do we do then, if we told somebody something we thought was right and discover it was wrong?"

"If we are strong, and they are near to us, we tell them what is right. If they are not near to us, we can't tell them that we were wrong, but we can teach ourselves to make sure that our own thinking is right before we say it – next time."

"I did not need to be old for you to tell me that, Papa."

Those words his father had spoken so many years before returned. Genes, his father had said. They govern us, in their own way.

At first, he hadn't appreciated what his father had been talking about; he'd been a twelve year old child. Maybe that was the reason why he hadn't placed any credence in his father's comments until his daughter, this child of his own, had somehow drawn it out of him.

Jeans were trousers, weren't they; hard working trousers? What had they to do with the behaviour of anybody's parents or past relatives?

He had thought that way for years until he noticed the different spelling in an article in a dentist's waiting room.

He'd laughed at his own stupidity. Jeans were on you, genes were in you. A bit of a joke there.

And what did twelve year old boys know about things that girls of a similar age were abysmally ignorant of? Did they know the difference between jeans and genes? Maybe they did. Maybe they didn't. He didn't know. His own daughter?

Well, she certainly knew the difference between some types of right and wrong.

He found a need to smile. "You asked me to start at the beginning."

She nodded her head. "I spoke too soon, didn't I? I have just taught myself something. I should have waited a bit."

"Yes." He squeezed her lightly, kissing the top of her hair. "That was the beginning. Now I will tell you about your Mumma, yourself and me. It is a long story but I will make it a short story."

"The good bits as well as the bad?"

"Yes. The important bits. Why your Mumma is in hospital and why I thought I would die last night. And when I thought I was going to die, many of the things that I have done and said that I told myself were right, I suddenly knew were wrong. And I wanted to live to tell you those things."

"I will listen like I am older, Papa."

"It's not going to be easy to tell you."

"Why?"

"Because you are so young."

"But I said I would be older while you tell me."

"You go to school with boys and girls the same age as you, don't you?"

"In my class, yes, but there are others."

"Of course, that was a bit silly of me. What I meant was the parents of the other children in your class are about the same age as each other - much younger mothers and fathers - much younger than me."

"Yes, most of them."

"When I married your mother, she was much younger than I was. I was old enough to be her father."

"You are my father, Papa. I am the lucky one."

He placed an arm around her and drew her close. "I will have to start again," he said, "so let me cuddle you."

She buried her cheek into the crook of his arm.

He thought for a few moments, gently running a hand over her hair as he did so, his mind seeking a passage through the tunnel; the tunnel of guidance.

"Before you were born, sweetheart, I met your mother."

She gave a brief titter, trying to look up, then speaking without doing so. "I told you, Papa, the bigger girls tell us things – lots of things. Maybe naughty things."

He returned a short laugh. "Very well – you win. I will now talk like the bigger girls who tell you things that you shouldn't know until you are bigger."

"But I have to know, Papa, for when I am bigger."

He smiled to himself and smoothed her hair again.

"But you are twelve years of age now."

"I know. But you were only twelve when you thought you were a man, Papa. You went fishing for your Mumma."

"Yes, sweetheart, but boys learn things younger than girls."

"How do you know, Papa, you have never been a girl? Girls learn things young, too, but they don't talk about it because they're not supposed to know. But the bigger girls tell us just like the bigger girls told them when they were younger."

A smile ran across his lips. It was a lost smile without a home because he had no mood for it.

He was delving into a sex talk with a twelve year old girl and that duty was for an older woman, surely. But if there were no older woman near enough to perform the duty, or willing to do it regardless, what did a father do?

Did he want a 'bigger girl' at the school to provide a lesson in the maturity of childhood? And what sort of lesson would it be if she agreed?

Before you were born, I met your mother, he had said. What an idiotic choice of words. Quite satisfactory if he were not her father – but he was her father. Uncle Ben, the doctor, had eliminated any doubt.

"Papa." Her words broke through his mental ramblings.

"Yes."

"You said you would start again."

"I was trying to decide the best way."

"Any way will do. I will listen to all of it."

"I have not been fair to your mother," he said slowly, holding her tightly so that she could not draw away from him.

"No, Papa, no. You are fair to everybody."

He shook his head, even though she could not see the movement of it. His thoughts had gone back a dozen years.

"When you looked through that little window and saw your Mumma with those other men, you saw them give her money, didn't you?"

"Yes. Some at the beginning and some at the end."

"Do you know what they call women who do those things for money?"

"Yes. There are lots of words. Do you want me to say them?"

"No. I never want to hear you say them."

"Why did you ask then?"

130

"It was part of telling you what you want to know. Why I blame myself."

"No, Papa, no. Mumma was laughing."

"Laughing is better than crying, sweetheart, and sometimes we laugh because we are crying inside."

"I never laugh when I am crying inside, like when I see Mumma."

"That is because you are twelve years of age, sweetheart."

"Yes, but you........"

"I know, I know," he interrupted, "but when I was twelve I had to work, to catch fish so that we could live. You are twelve and you go to school. You do not have to catch fish."

"But your fish are for all of us."

"Your Mumma did not have a father to catch fish. She had a mother, and the only thing your mother's mumma could do was what you saw your Mumma do."

He felt a tightening in the small body that he held to him. Looking down, he could not see the young eyes but he knew them of old. They would be sorting his words, putting them in the order of reality. Not seeing beyond her mind.

"And that is why Mumma does what she does?"

"At first, I think it was. The fishermen in this little village are not rich, sweetheart. Sometimes there are lots of fish in the nets and sometimes there are only a few. When the fishermen are married they do what you saw them do with your Mumma, with their wives, until they are quite old. But when they are not married, they look for girls who are not married. And they pay for what the girls let them do, but they don't have a lot of money to pay, so the girls who have no money don't ask for much. Enough for food and clothes that's all."

She pulled away so that her eyes could search his face. "But you caught the fish, Papa. You did not spend money on these girls. I know, I know. You were always near to me. I saw you fixing the nets, those things."

His arms drew her back. "I promised to tell you from the beginning. And that means I have to tell you the end."

"Will I like the end, Papa?"

"I hope you like the end, sweetheart, but I am frightened that you will not like me so much."

"I will always love you, Papa. I promise you I will. You have always talked with me."

"I hope so, I truly do."

Her head bent to kiss his arm that ran across her chest.

"When the men who are not married want to do the things that you saw, they want to do it with pretty girls if they can."

"Mumma is pretty."

"Yes, and she is young. Not young like you, but young to men like me. And when she was not much older than you, her own mumma did not get much money for the home. For food and the things we need."

There was a lull in the conversation, a heavy silence surrounded them. The fisherman let it dwell until his daughter spoke.

"So Mumma did these things for money, to help. With you?"

"Yes. At first."

"How old was she Papa?"

"Only eighteen."

"You did not love her?"

"Yes, I think I did love her - but love is a strange word. It is a little word that sometimes dies and at other times it grows bigger and bigger every day. We use it too much, I think. We say we love cakes and chocolates and flowers, and then we say we love a person. It is a much different kind of love when we say we love a person."

"Why?"

"Because we love the inside of a person, not the outside. We 'like' the pretty part on the outside, but it is the love for the inside of a person that grows bigger and bigger every day even though we can't see it. It grows in our memories. If we know that we want more of it, we know that our love for it is growing stronger. If we don't want more of it, it dies like the flowers we say we love before they wither, and the nice things that we say we love to eat, like chocolate. As soon as we swallow, it is gone."

"I always remember chocolate, Papa."

"Yes. But if you ate it every day it would always be the same memory. The memories that turn into love with people are the different things that grow bigger and more important every time we think of them."

"Like what?" She looked into his eyes.

"Yesterday, out on the water, I thought I might die and never see you again. I was frightened. Not frightened of dying, but frightened of not being here to tell you about the many little things that a father should tell his daughter as she grows older. And I thought about the walks we had together, the chats we had sitting on the beach wall, the building little sand castles and laughing when a wave came in and washed them away, those things; all different, but all good memories. Those things, sweetheart, that people do together, are the things that turn into love if their importance grows bigger and stronger in our minds; when they keep coming back to us."

Her head nodded slowly. "I think I understand, Papa, because I was frightened too. That was why I stayed on the wall when Uncle Ben came down to talk to me, to say it was better if I went home, because it was too dark to see anything. There were things that I wanted to say to you, too."

He kissed her cheek. "I'll bet it wasn't about chocolate." He tried to make light of her serious face.

"I could not eat anything while I waited."

"So you understand when I say that love of lots of things around us is very different to saying we love a special person. That love is inside like I said, we cannot see it or touch it."

Her head was nodding constantly as if she were absorbing his words, and her next words surprised him. "When did you know you loved Mumma?"

"When I saw you for the first time. She was feeding you."

"What did she say?"

"Nothing at first, she simply smiled at me. It was the most beautiful smile that I have ever seen. I can see it now. It said much more than words."

"But she did say something."

"Yes. She said it is a daughter for you, Paulo. When we were first together you were so kind to me I knew you had to have a daughter of your own."

"Why did she say that, Papa?"

"I don't know, I never asked her. But I think it was because life had been unkind to her. It was as if she wanted to present me with a gift and she had done it the only way she could."

"Gee, Papa." Tears flooded into the young eyes. "What did you say then?"

"I told your Mumma that I loved her, I truly loved her. I had never said those words to her before."

"Why? Why didn't you say that before?"

He paused, reflecting on the things he had said, and wondering, as he did so, whether or not he had already reached too far into the mind of a child. Eventually he said, "You told me that the bigger girls tell you things."

"Yes."

"Have they told you how not to have babies?"

"Yes. Lots of ways."

Lots of ways! So the bigger girls had told her lots of ways not to have babies if they were practising sex.

Did <u>he</u> know lots of ways for a girl to have sexual relations with a man and have the comforting knowledge that she would not fall pregnant? No, he didn't, not really. He knew the basic method of prevention but even that seemed to fail sometimes. The Catholic religion had a way of its own, too, or so he'd been told, but that seemed to have its short-comings.

But the bigger girls knew lots of ways, his twelve year old daughter had said.

All <u>he</u> knew at that moment was that he had to say something.

"You are twelve years of age and your Mumma was eighteen when I first met her."

"You told me that before."

"Yes. And I must now tell you something that you will not like to hear. I don't think you will love me because of it."

"I will always love you, Papa. Like you said, there are memories that we love – not the chocolate that is gone after we swallow it."

"Very well. It is this. When your mother first told me you were to be born, I was angry. She wanted you and I did not want you."

"She wanted me for you, Papa. You just told me."

"Yes, but I did not want you. I thought I was too old for children. I thought my whole life would be turned upside down."

"Was it turned upside down?"

"Yes," a smile creased his face. "In a wonderful way. In two wonderful ways, I think."

"Tell me."

"One way because when I saw you for that first time I thought you were the most wonderful present in the whole world. I was scared to touch you in case I broke a little toe off or something."

She tittered. "And what was the second thing?"

"I knew then that your mother truly loved me. I was not tricked like some of my friends thought. And that is what I thought, too. But when I saw you and the smile on your mother's face, I think I got tears in my eyes."

"There are tears in your eyes now, Papa."

He laughed, drawing a forearm across his cheeks. "So have you, sweetheart."

There were a few moments of silence between them before she said, "Is that the end of your story, Papa?"

"No. It is the middle. Do you want me to tell you more? You will not like all of it."

"Yes. I want to know. You must tell me like I am a bigger girl, because I have a story to tell, too."

"About the special room, is it?"

"Some, yes, some no. Some good and some bad, I think. But you finish first. I will listen properly."

"What I have to say is sad. It is sad because I did not care so much before, as I do now."

"Tell me."

"When you were a baby your mother did not take you to places where there were other babies."

"Why?"

"Because the other mothers did not want to talk to her. You know this is a fishing village. It is not big. Most people know what other people do."

"Like in the room you built before you built it?"

"Yes."

"But you took me for walks. The people stopped to talk to you, and to me."

"Yes. But some people are unkind. They don't know they are unkind. Gossip it's called. Telling stories about other people when they don't know the real story at all."

"Like who?"

"Like when a man is put in gaol for stealing something and they don't know why he stole it."

"Does it make a difference?"

"Yes, if he had no money and his children were starving."

"Did Mumma go to gaol for stealing something?"

"No, no. But I don't know how to tell a little girl."

"I said I would be a big girl when you talk to me, Papa."

He rubbed the butt of one palm across his eyes. "Very well, I will tell you the best way that I can. Your mother had a mumma who was hungry, so she did what she had to do to get food. That was how I first met her. And lots of people knew, so they wouldn't talk to her."

"But that's silly."

"Yes, I know. But we are all silly sometimes."

She gave a jerky laugh. "You are not silly, Papa. You talk to me like I am older because that is what I ask you to do."

"Then you will have to think older so that I can finish what I want to tell you. You will have to make your self know that I am serious with everything that I say."

"Can I ask if I do not understand?"

"Yes, of course. But no giggles."

She cuddled warm within his arms, aware of the strong aroma of fish on his clothing but not offended by it, and appreciating the security of his embrace. "I'm ready, Papa."

For a short time, he stroked her hair, thinking of how best to say what he promised to say, then he said; "The world is a strange place, sweetheart. It can be very unkind for a long time, then all of a sudden it is kind. And it can be the opposite."

"What was the most unkind thing that happened to you, Papa?"

"Being too old before you came into my life, before your mother gave you to me."

"And what was the kindest thing?"

He laughed spontaneously, as if she had outwitted his thoughts. "I've just told you. Seeing you for the first time."

"And what was the most unkind thing that happened to Mumma? Do you know?"

He was slow to answer, knowing that he was not privileged to answer, but that he should try. "You would have to ask your Mumma that, but if I'm allowed to guess, I think she would say that being so poor was the unkindest thing in her life."

"And what would have been the kindest thing in her life?"

"The same as me, I think. Having you."

"But she would not have had me if she hadn't met you. You would have had to come first." A knowledgeable smile lit her face as she looked up.

He laughed outright at her simple logic. "It seems that your mother and I shared you from the beginning, doesn't it?"

She did not know how to answer her father's question.

They were both silent. Gently he stroked her hair.

"Is that the end, Papa? I will tell you my story now."

"Oh, no, not yet. I have not told you about your mother. It is important. I have been unfair to her. I have acted like a fisherman when I have not been fishing. I have been unfair to your mother and I didn't know it. That is the worst part, not knowing how unfair I have been.

"Must you tell me?"

"Yes. It's important."

"Can you make it short? I don't think I am as old as I pretend to be."

"I'll try." He hesitated, as if uncertain of what was best to say, then he spoke softly, "When your Mother bought you home form hospital, we were both very happy. It was wonderful. But the money that I used to spend in the little 'bar' with my friends – the money that I thought I could save, was swallowed up by the things we had to get for you, so there was never any over."

"Did you need any over?"

"Yes, for you."

"For me." She drew away to look upwards. "I was only a baby, I didn't need money."

"No. Not then. But we knew that we had to put money aside for you later.

"Your mother wanted you to have good schooling. It was important to her – and me too."

"Oh."

"You go to a special school now, don't you? You wear a special uniform, you all meet down by the church and a bus calls to collect you, and bring you back in the afternoon. It is a different school from the one that is here."

"Yes."

"It is what they call a private school. It costs a lot more money than an ordinary school."

"How much more?"

"More than I make from my fish."

He knew from her silence that she had found the end to his story without him telling her.

She pushed his arm gently from her and stood from the seat. He had the sickening feeling that she was about to walk away from him, but instead, she turned and sat across his knees, one leg on either side and her eyes staring up into his own. "It is Mumma's money that pays for the special school. What we get from those goats and pigs and things I draw?"

"Yes. She made me promise not to tell you, but she is sick now and I had to break my promise. I will have to tell her."

"What did she say, Papa?"

"She said to me one night after you had gone to bed, she said, "We are not saving much money for our baby, Paulo, and you know I am not educated to get proper work. There are jobs in a few kitchens where the bachelors eat, but they are all taken. I am worried. I don't want her to grow up with no special training.""

"What did you say, Papa?"

"I said, I'm sorry. I said you know I go out earlier than the other fishermen and stay out later. What else can I do? I come home tired, I go to bed, I get up early and go out again."

"What did Mumma say?"

"I was working when I first met you, Paulo. I can get that job back again."

"What did you say, Papa?"

"I said, no, not that, never."

"What did Mumma say?"

"She said it has to be that, Paulo, or our lovely baby will have no future. The best she could hope for would be to marry a fisherman. And me, Paulo, do you know why I let you make me pregnant? Because you were the only man in all of them that I knew would be kind to me. All the others wanted to use me, that was all. You were never like that, Paulo."

"What did you say, Papa?"

"I did not say anything for two days. Not a word. I felt that I could not speak. I spoke to you but not to your Mumma."

"So how did it happen?"

"Your Mumma said – she said, "You must agree, Paulo, It is the only way. We have brought our baby into the world. We owe her something better than what we know might happen.""

"What did you say then, Papa?"

"I said it would be the end between your Mumma and me. I said I would not become one of the others."

"What did Mumma say then?"

"She looked into my eyes, sweetheart, like you are doing now. Then she said – you must build me a room of my own. I will never bring them into the house."

"And you built her that room. Where I see them sometimes?"

There was a silence between them.

"I am so sorry, so sorry," he finally said. "I have not been a good papa to you. I thought I was a man when I was only a boy, but now that I have told you this story, I don't think I have ever been a proper man at all."

"Why do you say that? Everybody likes you. Everybody thinks you are a proper man."

"For telling you that I let your Mumma do the things that she did."

"But it was for me."

"I know. But I should have done other things to make more money. When I was a young man, all I did with the money that my own Mumma did not need was spend it in the bar with my friends."

"But your books, Papa. You have those. You taught me proper reading and the meaning of words. The teacher asked me to stand at the front of the class and read to the others. I was proud; I was proud of you for teaching me."

"We cannot eat books, sweetheart."

"No, but it is books that teach us the things that get us the food to eat. The teacher said it."

He tried to laugh at the maturity of her comment. "You are talking like a bigger girl now. Am I making another mistake?"

She stood upright without apparent reason, as if uncertain with her thoughts; then she returned to her position across his knees once again. It was an odd action, her eyes perplexed, her fingers opening then tightening.

"No, Papa, you are wrong. You have always been teaching me. You are not making mistakes when you teach me. You don't say things that I don't know and expect me to know them. You ask me if I know. It has always been like that. You were that way with the books. You asked me if I remembered things. If I said no, you told me that I must read them again. You did not say that I was silly for not remembering."

"I could not do that. I had to read them more than once myself. My father was the real teacher. They were his books. I think I was stealing some of his words when I told you that good books are like poetry. When we read them for the second time we read words that we cannot remember reading the first time. Those were his thoughts. Look for the reason for those words, he said. Try to look into the writer's mind."

"Yes, Papa, your father taught you but he did not teach me. I did not know him. It was you who taught me. Books, you said, are brains. You said it lots of times. Get books into your head, you told me, and you will have brains in your head."

"That was a silly saying of mine. I have done many silly things."

"No, it was not silly, it gave me your birthday present."

"Birthday present?" His eyes were querying her comment but she did not enlarge on it.

Instead, she said, "What is it that made Mumma sick? Is it something she got from the men?"

"Yes."

"Can it be fixed?"

"Yes. In the big cities. Not here."

"Then she must go to the city."

He looked down, ashamed of what he must say. "I do not have the money."

"Is there no money left over after you pay the school?"

"Yes. There is some. That is where I have not been a proper man. I did not save the money that I wasted years ago. You said you cried when you looked through the little window and heard your mumma laughing. I heard her laughing too, and I wanted to cry. It hurt me but I could not cry. It was a different laugh that I heard; a false laugh, a pretend laugh, like when someone tells a joke that you don't understand. I knew it was my own fault. I should have done some other things, made more money so there was no need for her to do those things."

"But you did other things, Papa, when you put books in my head. And you said Mumma might have been crying inside."

"Yes. I know she was. I truly know she was crying inside."

She looked directly into her father's eyes, held her gaze for a moment, then slipped from his knees. "You still have your filthy clothes on. You will have to have a bath before we visit Mumma."

He stood. "Yes, and I will have to tell her that you know the story now. What I promised to never let you know."

"But I am a bigger girl now. I am always a bigger girl when you talk to me."

"It is nice of you to say that. I am ashamed of myself for how I have been. She will not like me anymore after she knows what I have told you."

"No, Papa, it is different. I watched through the little window. We must have a secret. I do not tell Mumma what you have told me and you do not tell her that I watched through the little window. You have taught me with the books, and Mumma has taught me grown-up things."

He glanced at her face; it was serious, without sign of impudent humour.

For a few moments they hugged each other before he kissed the top of her head and moved to bathe.

When he reappeared in readiness to attend the hospital, she was awaiting him.

He paused to stare at her. "That's a beautiful dress. When did you get it?"

"Mumma. My birthday."

"I have never seen it before."

"I have never worn it before. I thought I would never wear it." She gave a fleeting, timid smile. "I am a bigger girl now, papa. Last night I hated that dreadful storm but now I am so happy for it."

"Happy?"

"Yes. It gave us that long talk together. We know things now that we didn't know yesterday. Important things."

"Yes," he nodded. "Yes, we do, sweetheart. Every day is another day for learning. If we do not learn something new every day, no matter how small it is, I think we should stay in bed until tomorrow."

She laughed. "And Mumma must learn something new today, too. "

"What, especially what?"

"At the hospital you must tell her that money saved to help my schooling is for her to go to the city to be cured."

He shook his head. "I don't think she would ever agree to that. What she has done, she has done for you. It is to give you a better life than she had herself. It would be like her doing what she has done for nothing. She loves you too much for that to happen."

She smiled. I told you that I had something special to say to you, papa."

"Yes. You have done another painting."

"No. Not yet. But soon."

"What is it then?"

"I will have to give you your birthday present before it comes."

"Birthday present?"

Delight ran across her face. "I have won a scholarship. All of my school fees will be paid for the next five years. Mumma will not need to do what she is doing. Not any more. She can be with you and me all the time."

One palm came up to cover his eyes. "That – that is wonderful," he finally said. "Your Mumma will cry and cry and cry with happiness, but the whole time she will be laughing inside."

"Like you, Papa. You are crying outside now, but I hope you are laughing on the inside."

He hugged her. "I am just a silly fisherman. A silly, silly, fisherman who had to grow old before he knew that he was a man."

"No, Papa, but I think I will have to get some of the bigger girls at school to come and talk to you. They could teach you things about girls, I think."

He laughed, joyfully, brimming with a relief that he didn't fully understand. "I'm sure they could, I'm sure they could."

She saw his eyes drop to notice the carry bag that she held to one side, her sketching board and pencils poking out of the top.

"You are going to draw me again while I'm away."

"No. I am coming with you. I want to draw Mumma to hang in your bedroom."

"She will love that, I know. And I will destroy all of the others that she would not like."

"No. I will burn them. I want to watch them burn to nothing. But you must do something for me, Papa."

"Anything you ask, sweetheart."

"I want you to put another lock on that special room and keep the key for yourself."

"No. I built it and I will hate myself every time I look at it. I will pull it to pieces."

She ran into his arms, tears flowing from her eyes. "Papa," she said.

"Yes."

"Isn't it lovely to cry when you are so happy. I'm learning things I never knew. Important things."

"Yes." The word choked in his throat. For how many years of his life could a man remain stupid and void of understanding his opposite sex.

"Papa."

"Yes, sweetheart."

"I am the luckiest – the luckiest girl in the whole wide world for having such a lovely Mumma and Papa."

He couldn't reply. He couldn't speak. Dammit, he was thick with emotion.

Somehow, the rotten world that he thought he knew was not as rotten as it had so often seemed to be.

And there was always a future.

Nobody, just nobody, could take away the future.

Verses

Filton Hebbard

MY PEARL

Strolling through the garden
Taking time for tea
Holding hands together
That's just you and me

Sitting in the movies
Cuddling in the dark
Feeding baby ducklings
Together in the park

Dancing at the disco
Watching funny lights
Boys in vulgar tee shirts
Girls in sexy tights

Kissing in the parlour
Weak as weak can be
Feeling rather foolish
Glad no-one can see

Wishing I was married
Just like Mum and Dad
There's much more in loving
Than fun I've ever had

But knowing there's a reason
For my true kind of girl
As in that bed of oysters
I know I'll find my pearl.

NO FOOL LIKE AN OLD FOOL

The maid was young and pretty
Though very short of learning
Her master's wife was in the earth
So for her he had a yearning

She'd left her school at fourteen years
To help an ailing mother
And what her basic training lacked
She learned not from her brother

She failed to sound her aitches
Except when they were quiet
And though she gorged on sickly foods
She had no need to diet

She'd waltz into her master's room
With breakfast on a tray
And scarcely out of bed herself
He'd palpitate all day

He'd travelled 'cross all oceans
And white now was his hair
But thought with all fine breeding
He sought this maiden fair

At night-time by the flickering hearth
She'd sit naive and bold
As he with tone and eloquence
Adventures would unfold

He though that with his culture true
He'd get this lass in arms
She'd take it as a part of work
To melt before his charms

She'd stretch out in her night attire
like child not yet at school
And he would see the form of her
An old man made a fool

He spoke on joys of marriage
Deep thrill of nuptial bliss
And wide-eyed she moved closer
Dear master I'm your miss

He took her to his boudoir
Where simple-like she said
They say your wife had jewellery
That bedecked all her head

And quickly to impress her
She'd chosen moment well
He opened secret jewel box
Of treasures he'd not sell

She tried a necklace beautiful
Hands trembling at the sight
Then walked out on the terrace
And romanced on the night

He hastened swiftly to her side
And she gave him lingering kiss
Desire seemed to hide from him
How transformed was this miss

She put the necklace back in box
To ease his clear alarm
Then clinging very close to him
She led him by the arm

That night he had a student
A dux of Eros fame
For she did withhold nothing
Till energies were lame

And in the morning with the dawn
She still slept by his side
Though he left surreptiously
His jewellery to hide

Alas it was all missing
He searched in panic state
Whilst blissfully within his bed
There dozed a costly mate

Come wakening she was again
A child quite immature
She rushed to prepare breakfast
For a master now with cure

He searched all nooks and crannies
She joined with vacant talk
They even shook their slippers out
For jewellery can walk

Now even though that master
Was heavy with suspect
His maid was spared the gendarmes
Least he lose his respect

She had a perfect alibi
And said she'd tell them all
She'd clung to him so ever tight
In fear from bed she'd fall

Though she did leave his service
Not many weeks from that
And lived a life of luxury
With a slim man called the Cat.

Filton Hebbard

NO ONE BUT YOU

I think of you my darling
    alone by my side
That pathway to heaven
    each day I do ride
The touch of your sweet lips
    the toss of your hair
I see oh so clearly
    even when you're not there
The longing to hold you
    to know you are mine
Is something my poor heart
    calls passion divine
So don't stay away dear
    come back very soon
The sky is all darkness
    the nights have no moon
And I'll keep on waiting
    I'll be ever true
I'm saving my loving
    for no one ----simply no one
    --------- but you.

OLD FRIENDS

Some of the richness that we lose
    as life slips slowly by
Is the joy of treasured friendship
    when souls make journeys high
How often in those pensive moods
    when we think of our mates
Do we wish we'd been kinder
    this side of heaven's gates
But now that they have left us
    far-gone from real touch
Let's hope that they learn somehow
    that we cared very much
For in this world of hassle
    where it's catch-if-catch-you-can
We often fail so badly
    with our love for fellow man
But they are not forgotten
    old friends who've passed away
May we have chance to make amends
    when comes our Judgement day.

Filton Hebbard

OUR WORDS OF CONSOLATION

To be a human one must suffer
    said the aged man
How can we understand the moods
    for empty we began
If we have not packed into us
    from vacant babies minds
Those tempests of emotions
    where living is unkind

To say we know the feelings
    of a man who hates another
Is like the one who ridicules
    the passions of a lover
Unless the need to love or hate
    has been a known torment
The fool who casts opinion
    should ever more lament

To play the part benevolent
    and understand with balm
The anguish of an aching heart
    we have but oily palm
Unless we know with honesty
    that we have felt that way
And our words of consolation
    are real ghosts of yesterday.

OUT IN THE COUNTRY

Out in the country
    where life is true
Where the air is fresh
    and the skies are blue
That's where I long
    to finish my days
Where nature is freed
    from the world's many plays
To sit 'neath the trees
    as I sat when a child
Where the birds are all free
    and the plants are all wild
Alone with my thoughts
    on the troubles of Man
Where the cities are shadows
    of how life began
That's where I long
    and that's where I'll be
Where the birthright is freedom
    to all that I see
Yes, out in the country
    where life is true
Out in the country
    but thinking, still thinking of you.

Filton Hebbard

PAINS OF MATURITY

There is a painful barrier
Placed in those early years
Our numbers are quite limited
Who pass it without tears

That barrier comes after school
With adulthood in birth
Before we gain maturity
Some laughter has false mirth

We burst with inhibitions
And lack a certain poise
Until we capture polish
Our thoughts disturb like noise

It's in this mixed up thinking
That some resort to drugs
Some girls find prostitution
Some boys make desperate thugs

It is a warped society
Foundations laid on silt
What child can take its pressures
Without some kind of wilt

Some youngsters grope for sedatives
Some others for wild kicks
Was living always quite this bad
What are theses modern tricks

What drives our kids to this abuse
They must know what's in store
Feed metal to a magnet
It always longs for more

Now writhe you broken child
Destroyed yet scarcely born
Your mother was a gently soul
She nursed you from each morn

To see you chuckle with your toys
To stack them row on row
What crazy speculation
This way could see you grow

Why did you take those tablets
Sure you had growing pains
But every man before you
Has known those youthful strains

It's true the pressures of this age
Are greater than before
But so are opportunities
They've increased by the score

Perhaps it is the freedom
That you think is your right
The hand of all your fathers
Has lost much of its might

Your voice was heard too early
You chose the kind of jam
There used to be a parliament
Shaped like your own white pram

And it is somewhat terrible
That life so dear and sweet
Could sink when scarcely floated
Before you grew men's feet.

Filton Hebbard

PANTY HOSE

King Arthur's big round table
Was full of handsome knights
They rode great horse to battle
In ballerina tights

They were the predecessors
Of modern panty hose
Cromwell came years later
But his were on the nose

So you sweet with-it ladies
Dressed in your mini-skirts
Wear trousers that belonged to men
In the days of iron shirts

Now don't think I'm suggesting
That you protect your chest
The next best thing to panty hose
Is see-through voile breast

So keep on learning girlies
Your fashions are divine
Three cheers for ancient history
Where was Eve's washing line.

PARTNERS FOR EVER

I am for you, dear
You are for me
Partners for ever
That's what we'll be

We'll walk down the pathway
Of what they call life
A ring on your finger
That makes you my wife

Sometimes we'll differ
On our point of view
But isn't that proper
With everything new

We'll shoulder the storm clouds
And welcome the sun
We'll share any troubles
As well as the fun

But when we grow older
And our hair turns to gray
We'll have all those memories
Of true love when we say

I am for you, dear
You are for me
Partners for ever
That's what we'll be

Filton Hebbard

PASSING FRIENDS

They came and worked, from dawn till dusk
Their gardens filled with flowers and musk
They lifted, that dark standard home
To a picture piece, through books you'd comb
But then a sign loomed brazen clear
And neighbours knew, the end was near
For no man with a family love
Can wait for help, from up above
He has to take each step in line
Or simply wither on the vine
As ladders are for one and all
So man must climb, but never fall
And when they go, as go they will
The fondest thoughts will linger still
And I shall with my inner eye
See them, clear, until I die.

PATHOS

We feel the pain of anguish
    in that sometimes lonely road
As we move our lives through childhood
    to an adult's family load
There are happenings so pointless
    in the scorn of fellow man
Who seek a chance to ridicule
    a project we began
Our playing fields of yesterday
    are slowly put to rest
When the energies we gave them
    begin to fail the test
And we look into the future
    of our worn and aching bones
As we try to muster pleasure
    from old photos void of groans
We tell ourselves that middle age
    shall be a time of joy
As our children will no longer seek
    the latest costly toy
We think that we have suffered much
    to take our place in life
As a man looks at his family
    embracing his fond wife
But then we walk that lonely road
    musing on our grief
Of all the things we could have done
    if time were not a thief
And with the kindly tolerance
    that we think that we have shown
We see a lady push a pram
    with a baby newly grown
So we stop to pass a kindly word
    and exercise our charm
But what we see both snug and warm
    fills us with alarm
For the baby's eyes are rolling
    as defective as its mind
And we all wrapped in pathos

no proper words can find
But the lady gives a timid smile
and says in softened tone
I love my darling little boy
he's all I'll ever own.

PLANS

How lonely was that darkened night
    as he sat in the window light
The water sparkled far away
    and Sun had stolen off with day
The city blocks were rearing high
    their lights far-stretching in the sky
Around him was a wondrous land
    of couples strolling hand-in-hand
Yet he was lonely and a fool
    he'd set himself in ridicule

He'd had a castle in his plans
    that reached right out to other lands
For he'd been guided by a force
    that ended in a deep remorse
He'd tried to show his only star
    a path in life that would not mar
The fragrance of her quality
    that was not clear for men to see
And in his foolishness it seems
    he put an end to all his dreams

For with anxiety to scheme
    to build he thought a better team
He'd gone headlong in too fast
    his ship at sea soon lost it's mast
For reading in between each line
    is best if left to power divine
For guessing tends to spoil a man
    and bring destruction to good plan
For others too are prone to guess
    and what was tidy turns to mess

Though if a thing is meant to be
    to place itself in destiny
The early pitfalls are not bound
    forever after it to hound
Too much is gained, he did declare
    when troubles rise to clear the air

159

For after they have done their task
    the guessing then has lost its mask
And each sees clear where troubles laid
    then love is lost or love is made.

PLEASE

Please------------believe in me
    that's all I ask
My----------------love flows free
    it's not a task
Come--------------to my arms
    they are for you
I'll----------------hold you close
    that's what I'll do
So----------------darling please
    don't turn away
My---------------anxious heart
    has much to say
When-----------you are near
    I feel so grand
My---------------head is high
    I own the land
So----------------darling please
    believe in me
You--------------are the one
    you're all I see
Please, please, believe in me
    I love you so.

PRETTY WOMAN

Pretty woman, pretty woman
Pretty woman by my side
Pretty woman, pretty woman
I know that you have lied
You didn't spend last evening
With your mother dear
For I can see within your eye
There is a guilty tear

Pretty woman, pretty woman
Why did you do this thing
You have upon your finger
A treasured golden ring
Was there a special reason
For you to act this way
I said that I would love you
Forever and a day

Pretty woman, pretty woman
I don't know what to do
Should I hear alarm bells ringing
Or keep my faith in you
I never thought the time would come
When you would need another
It's tearing at my anxious heart
Am I a hopeless lover

Pretty woman, pretty woman
I'm kind of sick inside
Last night when your mother rang
I think I could have died
She asked if she could have a word
And I said you weren't home
I couldn't say my darling girl
Was somewhere on the roam

Pretty woman ------- what am I to do
Pretty woman ------- I'm in love with you.

QUIET KID WITH MANNERS

Sudden surge of power
Back wheels madly spin
Grip the steering lightly
In the race to win

Listen to the engine
Hear it scream to pitch
Be careful with the gears
And ever-present ditch

Sweep around the corner
Eyes upon the track
Mighty motor roaring
Pressure on the back

Straighten up wide open
Prickle with the thrill
Toss the pebbles sidewards
Crest that sun-kissed hill

Down into the gully
Blurred faces on the fence
Steering hard into the bend
Round it in suspense

Hard upon the throttle
Smell the rubber burn
Watch that crazy driver
Tense now for the turn

Away again like lightning
Home straight coming up
One lap now of twenty
Then the golden cup

Someone's on the tail
Mustn't let him pass
Crowd the inner circuit
Hug the battered grass

Body wet and clammy
Underwear all damp
What's that madly waving
Pointing at the ramp

Stop and lose position
When holding number one
Sorry couldn't see it
Give her extra gun

Smoke now sending signals
Difficult to see
Be careful on the switch back
You'll catch a sturdy tree

Then suddenly it's over
Chequered flag is down
Laughter mixed with tears
You fool, you bloody clown

Control that pent emotion
Garland round that neck
Good luck is someone's mentor
Top card in the deck

Now take the highway homeward
Steady as a rock
Courtesy with signals
Thirty on the clock

Shy wave then to neighbours
Puzzled are their nods
Quiet kid with manners
King of all hot rods.

REFLECTIONS AND COMING HOME

The wind across the tarmac swirled
So cold and laced with rain
No pleasure for a tired man
To seek that aeroplane

Then take off in a thunderous roar
To surge up in the sky
The roof tops falling down below
And firmament so high

To witness blue of ocean
Wave caps of snowy white
The hinterland so ominous
But coastline sheer delight

The sparkle on the waterways
The snake-like river streams
Somewhere behind those window panes
That girl of all my dreams

Those are the things that filled me
As I refreshed my soul
With what my eyes could bring me
When wingtips formed a roll

O'er land I then did traverse
Green rugged mountain sides
Were right down there beneath me
So far from heaving tides

Then plateaus came and slipped away
The patchwork quilt of farms
With isolated homesteads
All parched with rainless qualms

Cloud banks took out my vision
The world was not in sight
I climbed right up beyond it
Oh lovely sun of light

Those clouds were then a carpet
A bed of fairy floss
They rolled on to eternity
Like stones that grow no moss

I now was in another world
A blanket on my past
The pilot held my destiny
Perhaps the die was cast

Should I not walk on earth again
To say a tender word
Why had I said those foolish things
So better quite unheard

But then the flight was over
The sun fired all the West
Red dust in up-drawn currents
Was sanguine in its zest

The bushland closed in darkness
Vague coastline silhouette
But in that jewel-lit Sydney
Was my dear Mignonette

The winding streets were dazzling
A million jumping stars
With probing beams of headlight
From moving motor cars

So beautiful it was that scene
Of Sydney from the sky
When heaven fell upon it
As sunlight had to die

I wished I had religion
So I could kneel and pray
To ask the Lord for many years
Before my judgement day

For I would use them wisely
I'd foster tender mood
And all the foolish things I'd done
Would not seem quite so rude

Then I would land some other day
From out those heavens high
To greet not winds of iciness
But girl of sparkling eye

And I would hold her close to me
Feel love in soft warm lips
And know the past was over
Forgiven were my slips.

Filton Hebbard

REFLECTIONS IN DRINK

Dark ripples on the water
White yachts passing by
That is what I'm watching
From my window three floors high

The sky is blue though hazy
And sun with August chill
The urge to stretch for bottle
Is testing all my will

A speedboat forms a pattern
The creamy bubbling wake
Like frosting making messages
On someone's birthday cake

Birds are seeking foodstuffs
Not far out from the land
Thank heavens for the larder
A few feet from my hand

There goes the harbour ferry
The plimsoll near the blue
A host of happy people
Taking in the view

Rising stark quite near me
Dried sticks of winter tree
Though with the joy of springtime
Green leafage should I see

I could go on forever
With this void and vacant talk
But now I reach for bottle
It never learnt to walk.

REFLECTIONS ON LOVE

Love
> How fickle you can be
> No man beyond his wishes
> Ever can he see

Love
> A sense we can't define
> Yet ever through the ages
> You take your place with wine

Love
> A sort of blind man's buff
> You pull like heavy magnet
> Until you've had enough

Love
> The cruellest, kindest thing
> A fountain built on tears
> Even though you make heart sing

Love
> Why don't you come in pairs
> Then happiness would blossom
> Each one would know who's theirs.

Filton Hebbard

RELIGION

What has religion done to us, has it been right or wrong
We go to church with deep respect and sing a mournful song

But outside in the wilderness of what we call God's land
We take up arms and massacre in a scale that is quite grand

We have a marvellous choice of creeds like in a market square
And should we fill with discontent a hundred more are there

We'll always find a pious soul to tell us we were right
When we embraced another creed to guide us with its Light

We bow and kneel and genuflect, and sometimes kiss the ground
To please the Lord who's looking down, at the not-so-very, merry-go-round

It's fair to wonder what He thinks of all the things we do
As proving our choice is the best, all others do we hew

For we make up a set of rules on how we should behave
And the one who does not follow it, is a hapless, stupid knave

But when we get to heaven, if that's what we might do
And wives have had two husbands and husbands, wives a few

We'll all convert to Mormons for they might have it right
And fighting in the day time, will then bring joy at night.

REMINISCING

I love to lie at night-time
When the sun has sunken low
An think of all my happenings
Before to sleep I go

I journey to my childhood
With all its daily schemes
Of sailing on forever
In the lugger of my dreams

I thought I'd get a sailing boat
The world would be my home
I'd laugh at all life's troubles
As on and on I'd roam

But nothing ever came of that
As madmen made a war
And in that crazy fracas
I had to be for sure

And somehow I survived it
With fortunes kindly grace
So back to school for learning
A new life then to face

Amongst all indecisions
A marriage came my way
And I resigned my happenings
To steady day-by-day

But each man has a destiny
A certain kind of soul
It cannot lie forever
In the depths of any hole

So one night in my pensiveness
Whilst gazing through my mind
I knew I had to journey
For happiness to find

Filton Hebbard

Not happiness of fleshpots
For those I had in score
But happiness of childhood
When Hitler closed the door

For there must be a reckoning
When man is put to test
If he has got a character
Or chicken in his chest

So I decided on my couch
That ere my span had been
I'd not forsake my childhood
Until its dreams I'd seen

Then they could lay me gently
In that fancy velvet box
With future in eternity
As screws were used for locks

And with my breath begone me
Blue eyes of worthless sight
I'd then have earned my freedom
To meet that endless night.

RUNNING BACKWARDS

Now I sit all alone by the roadside
    my thoughts running back through the years
I think of the love and the laughter
    then my mind turns to pathos and tears

They say life's a wonderful journey
    it sorts out the men from the boys
That girls are the pathway to heaven
    men must cherish, not use them as toys

So now I must live with the heartache
    of knowing how foolish I've been
For choosing a pathway of pleasure
    quite blind to what I've not seen

But I wonder, if I could run backwards
    to have all those years once again
Would I be quite as foolish
    and take joy as life's answer to pain

For we cannot be blamed for behaviour
    that grew from the genes of our birth
And what passed down the line of ancestors
    is the good and the bad of our worth.

SAD SENTIMENT

They lived within the confines
Of a station in the bush
The husband was a quiet man
Who lacked all city push

He rounded sheep and cattle
And rode the boundary fence
A few clothes and his saddle
Were his limit to expense

His pay was just the usual
He failed to warrant more
His wife received the all of it
He'd not let her look poor

She had a streak of coloured blood
An eighth or quarter caste
It gave her sex attraction
For affairs that do not last

Whenever he went riding out
For days sometimes on end
She'd go uptown a-shopping
And all his money spend

She too lacked finer breeding
That keeps all morals right
So without sense of loyalty
She erred sometimes at night

Her dull though kindly husband
Thought she was of the best
He'd never come home suddenly
Or put her to the test

Sometimes when he was riding fence
As lonely as the sky
He'd think of simple things to do
Before came time to die

The main thought was a cottage
Red brick and cosy warm
Though rain and sun could weather him
She'd shelter from all storm

The boss might find the money
If her promised work for life
And this wide world held nothing
Too good for his dear wife

With saddle as his pillow
He'd watch those twinkling lights
He smugly thought of oldsters
Saying marriage was all fights

He had a type of privacy
Two rooms built on the barn
But next door was the doss house
Where the bachelors spun yarn

This wasn't quite the nicest place
When drinking was in bout
Liquor raised most voices
At times all things came out

He packed his gear one Tuesday
To check the pastures east
He said he'd try for Friday
Though it took four days at least

A snap storm came on Wednesday
And marooned a flock of sheep
He urgently required help
And rode home without sleep

He thought this sense of duty
Might please his wealthy boss
To build a little cottage
Was not half the pending loss

The soft ground dulled the hoof beats
Cushioned by the rain
How wonderful would be the joy
To hold his wife again

He struck a match excitedly
As he stepped through the door
But God those clothes were not his own
Thrown loosely on the floor

A pair of startled faces looked
And saw him in the gloom
A shocked and ghostly silence
Was the echo in that room

The match burnt to his fingers
Though he didn't feel the pain
And soon as he found movement
He stepped back to the rain

His whole wide world was empty
Could women never learn
Though men may feel mixed passions
For faithfulness they yearn

Though women can with graded ease
Forgive their men who stray
A man can't lose the picture
That his mind sees every day

Half-dazed he went back to his horse
And let it feed a while
Then without wakening his boss
He rode back mile on mile

He swam his horse to join the sheep
Now crowded neck on neck
Then slapped it on the buttocks
With a tired 'get to heck'

He saw the torrents rising
And he knew the sheep would drown
But they were due for slaughter soon
The trucks were in the town

He's never ever learnt to swim
He too they found next day
And they laid him on a wagon
In a bed of softened hay

So his wife was given sympathy
From all who knew her spouse
Though she ended in the city
Where a Madam ran a house

And she died amongst the vermin
Of a dirty little room
Which was far below the visions
Of a plain though honest groom.

Filton Hebbard

SEAGULLS

I watched those birds
those seagulls swooping
round and round
So white and clean
they seemed to be
and confident
Gliding low across
that angry sea
Dipping down unto
the heaving swell
Then lifting high
with gracious charm
no sign of fear of nature's harm
Just seeking food
the fish that tumbled
in that frothy foam
for little ones perhaps
high up within
a cliff-side home

But me
no answer have I found
to satisfy my thoughts
about that angry sea
for it puts terror in my veins
Yet those small birds
viewed it with contempt
as if from nature's will
they were exempt
But they feared me
and never would I hurt
those handsome birds
I threw them crumbled bread
so often on the shore
they fluttered
terrified it seemed
of coming close
a friendly lifted arm

and they'd be off
away from needless harm

What is it then
about this world
of ours
when every living soul
has need to fear
Some creatures big
and others small
but fears are there
for one and all
Do those small seagulls
have it right
Have they
from lofty regions high
as they look down
from sunlit sky
see madness down below
where trust melts
faster than a summer snow

I think they have
I truly think they have
for when I lift
my harmless arm
to throw breadcrumbs
in movement kind
they fear me
Yes
they do not trust
a living thing
even when they hear it sing

Nature
the sea itself
they have no fear of it
no oily palm
is stretched to greet
No rustle in the grasses high
no vicious claws up in the sky

no secret plans to undermine
Just nature
giving its all
Fight it if you wish
or if you can
Well
what you see is what you get
those seagulls
they do not seek recall
or passions vet
they've learnt to trust
no living thing at all.

SEE THE WORLD AS I DO

See the world as I do
Take it in your stride
Laugh at all your troubles
Don't hold them tight inside

Walk along the highway
Give a friendly wave
Love is meant for sharing
Not a thing to save

Be the kind of person
Who meets you at the door
With arms that are wide open
Now who could ask for more

I have an urge of passion
To rid the world of pain
And fill it all with kisses
Not once, but time again

So darling let me hold you
I want you in my arms
To feel my heart pounding
As I take in your charms

And when the world is older
We'll both be older too
And the things I said in courting
I'll say again to you

Some people think that heaven
Is up there in the sky
But I say real heaven
Is right here where we lie

So darling don't be angry
At things I sometimes do
For I will always love you
With love that's very true

Just see the world as I do
Take it in your stride
Laugh at all your troubles
Don't hold them tight inside.

SHARING

Once upon a garden seat
There sat a man and miss
And feeling rather naughty
He gave to her a kiss

She looked at him intently
Her eyes all soft and blue
Now any male this reading
Has such occurred to you

He didn't know if she were bad
Or if she thought it good
And if good were her thinking
Was it good that he could

He suffered mixed emotions
Should next he touch her knee
It was a hard decision
Get ready then to flee

But brave unto his action
He saw the sweetest smile
Give mercy to his courage
He knew he'd stay a while.

Filton Hebbard

SHE SINGS LITTLE SONGS

She walks down the street like a princess
Her figure is something divine
The whistles from boys never reach her
For she said that she'd always be mine
The smile that she gives is exciting
My heart races like it's downhill
If you knew the way that she kisses
You'd never get over the thrill

For my baby is a sensation
A type of a two-legged charm
And I am as proud as a peacock
When she couples into my arm
She sings little songs when we're walking
Happiness flows from each word
I marvel at where she has found them
They make music that I've never found

And all of the sweetness in honey
Is lemon to my darling girl
She tosses her hair when she's laughing
My thinking is all in a whirl
So I put you men at full notice
Don't try to take my girl from me
She's as true as the blue of the ocean
As even a blind man can see.

SHRUNKEN LIFE

Our life is three score years and ten
Statistics so allow
Which means that those born that span ago
Should not be with us now

So Grandpa what a damn fool thing
You let your mother do
She should have withheld passion
To postdate life for you

There's no sense being born too soon
For each start has an end
Just mark yourself up seventy
And hope you've made a friend

It might seem lots of living
To a child with chores to do
But when it's halfway over
Those years seem just too few

For of those allocated years
We sleep about a third
That leaves say forty seven
To listen and be heard

Now if we count our schooling
The same as if at work
With transport ten hours go each day
These duties do not shirk

Then say that breakfast's hardly fun
And luncheon not much more
Link two hours with the other ten
That's twelve from twenty four

There goes full half the forty seven
That we are wide awake
So twenty four if generous
Are getting near the cake

Filton Hebbard

But who can count the first five years
Come tell what happened then
Though I pride distant memory
Before five I've short pen

And though we stretch to seventy
Let's look at sixty five
Are we great healthy joyful brutes
Or only part alive

So if we take those first two five years
The first and final few
From that last count of twenty four
I'm sweating now – are you.

SINEWS WITHOUT SALT

When shipwrecked on an island
Where cannibals were rife
The man built far in treetop
A home for self and wife

She thought the climb was needless
Why was it up so high
He hadn't told her what he knew
Of two-legged cottage pie

He thought that if she fattened
On all the island fare
Though cannibals might savour her
For him they would not care

So he would catch her tender duck
And wild pigs stun a few
Whilst she'd loll back most gracefully
To watch him barbecue

He fed her large size portions
Which she ate with a will
The waist line she once cherished
She now seemed keen to fill

He swung about the branches
In man-made monkey style
And she with understanding
Suppresses her ready smile

When she at last grew heavy
And could not reach tree top
He built her shelter on the ground
Though climbing he'd not stop

But he awoke one morning
To find the sharpest spear
Within the grasp of cannibal
Was tickling at his ear

He pointed at his skinny legs
Tough sinew of his arms
And indicated that below
Was girl of bistro charms

They simply prodded him with point
And forced him to the ground
Where much to his astonishment
No fattened wife was found

They dragged him to a village
And to his deep concern
He saw the making of a fire
Beneath a monstrous urn

And sitting there upon the sand
Legs crossed beside the chief
Was wife of plump proportions
Bedecked in one fig leaf

He called for some assistance
And got her friendly wave
Tree tops were built for monkeys
He should have tried a cave

For she also had learning
Girls too can read a book
Most natives like fat women
And all men like a look

So she had at a chosen time
Made bare her what-yer-call
And men of any colour
For that most times would fall

For logical is thinking
That says I love you too
In preference to thickening
A bowl of native stew

Though later with her rescue
She said her greatest fault
When helping eat her husband
Was meat so void of salt.

Filton Hebbard

SOMEWHERE UP AHEAD

The night has many blessings
That's where we learn to think
Of how the chain of destiny
Each day forms further link

The evening lets us ponder
Without a blatant squeal
As the pincers of life's troubles
Grip our Achilles' heel

When dusk does come to soften
The hardness of our day
And music fans the breezes
As the sun sinks far away

The troubles that tomorrow brings
Are not within the mind
And we are sewing memories
Of what we've left behind

Sometimes we build a daisy chain
With thoughts of someone fond
But hasn't life already taught
To look not far beyond

For there shall come the dawning
It happens every night
And kind though be the virtues
Of evenings without light

There always is our destiny
That's somewhere up ahead
And the links we build by daylight
to our evening chain are fed.

STAY CLOSE

Stay close please don't leave me
Take hold of my hand
I feel so uncertain
Do you understand

I've always been lonely
I have no true friends
I seem to offend them
Then can't make amends

I've longed for a sweetheart
To treasure and hold
But I haven't the courage
I've never been bold

I shake at your presence
I feel such a fool
I'm awkward and clumsy
Am I donkey or mule

But I could be different
I know I could learn
It's only some teaching
That's what I yearn

Stay close please don't leave me
Take hold of my hand
I feel so uncertain
Do you understand.

SUSTENANCE

What happens to the thinking
Of those who reach such power
As to make our regulations
From their cushioned ivory tower

They tell us that employers
Must now set cash aside
To accommodate the final years
Of those who've not yet died

Our social service system
They say with accents clear
Is becoming over-laden
With our loved ones, very dear

So employers now, not Parliament
Will have to bear the load
As the short-brains we elected
Continue with their goad

For they cannot seem to see the end
Of the system they have made
Where unemployment has grown high
As if with devils' spade

Technology is introduced
To play its special part
In making sure that basic skills
Are a disappearing Art

Our children think computers
Are all there is to know
As houses that their forebears built
From packet seed must grow

Now if we keep our migrant take
That boosts the politician
Our parents who from childhood toiled
Will die from malnutrition

For we are moving to a world
Where trades will soon be lost
And employers who paid workers
Will minimise the cost

Some children now will never work
And live upon the dole
Then marry to seek happiness
In their God-forsaken role

And they'll also have children
With energies to spare
And not have need to regulate
As they'll get child care

For these supposed scholars
Who govern our fair land
Are leading us to wilderness
With their palliative hand

And how can our employers
Plan pensions for their staff
Who've had to join the dole queues
Where security's a laugh.

SWEET AS ANYTHING

Sweet as anything
    that's what you are

Always on my mind
    both near or far

When I close my eyes
    I see you clear

Open them again
    and hide a tear

Love is what I have
    for only you

Darling please believe
    it's ever true

When you are away
    I miss you so

What a fool I was
    to let you go

With my aching heart
    I now must say

Darling on my knees
    come back to stay

Please please please
    come back to stay.

TENDERNESS

There are kisses on my lips for you
There is loving in my heart that's true
There is romance in my mind
If only I could find
The one my dreams are calling to

There is tenderness beyond extreme
There's caressing with an endless theme
There is softness in my touch
For the one I love so much
If only she would walk out of my dream

There were moments I recall with thrill
There was warmth as we embraced so still
There were tears within my eyes
As dawn revealed my lies
And told me that our dreams do not fulfil

So may I compromise some way
Stretch out my arms and simply say
If I am not the best
I'll try harder than the rest
Please come into my heart one day

Please come into my heart
Come alive and let us start
Please come into my heart one day.

Filton Hebbard

THAT LONELY FEELING

I can't explain that lonely feeling
It is with me every day
It is with me in the night-time
It simple will not go away

I close my eyes and see you clearly
You are laughing with the world
Your face is filled with sparkle
By a spirit so unfurled

When I stretch my hand to touch you
Knowing that you are not there
I wonder at my madness
As my fingers stroke your hair

I am nothing but a dreamer
A foolish man without a brain
For I know I'm seeking something
That I'm sure I'll never gain

For love seems to allude me
Though it basks my friends in joy
And I am on the outside
Like a child's broken toy

And I wonder if the reason
Is because I am so shy
But that's how nature made me
I can't change it when I try

So if there is a partner
Who feels the way I do
Please come into my heart strings
I'll do anything ---- just anything ---- for you.

THE ANIMAL IN ME

I saw you walking by the waterfall
    I saw you talking to a chimp
I saw the alligator smile at you
    and puff like a blimp

I saw the elephant nod kindly
    I saw the hippo give a wink
I saw the tiger show his famous teeth
    and the time for me to think

For if animals within the zoo
    could love you in that way
Why can't the animal in me
    join you in lover's play

For honey I'm a cuddly bear
    who'd make you oh so warm
I could take you to my little den
    and show you all my form

I could let the monkey out of me
    and prove that I'm no wolf
I could treat you ever tenderly
    so shy but not aloof

You could be my purring pussy cat
    to stroke and call my own
To keep out of the human zoo
    as mine and mine alone

So don't walk by the waterfall
    or talk to hairy chimps
I'll carry you through thick and thin
    you'll not see any limps

I'm not a lion in a den
    or a monkey in a tree
For if I knew a million girls
    it's only you I'd see

197

Filton Hebbard

I'm not a real cuddly bear
    or something from a zoo
I'm just a normal fellow
    who has much love for you.

THE LOSING GAME

He looked into her face
And saw her smiling lips
Her slender nose
The smooth fine texture
Of her creamy skin
The contrast of her bright
And sparkling eyes
Against the dark hair clustering
In contour of her head
    And hello there, she said

He longed to take her
In his arms and care
Not for the passing world around
As he would say in truth
The many tender things
That often flowed through his mind
And with the urge
To speak those words
He always fought
    Though this is what he thought

He knew she was the essence
Of the girl for whom
He'd always longed
So truly feminine
And yet so personally firm
So very warm and close
But angry if the need arose
For she had character that he admired
    Fighting himself he tried

He hesitated with his voice
Not from lack of fortitude
But from the spoken words
Of yesterday
The agony of pride
The crime of honesty today
That lacks a modern niche

The deep embarrassment of saying
This is heaven this is hell
    How could this girl he tell

He wanted much
To have her always near
To share the countless happenings
Of life
Both good and bad
To reminisce on foolish things
To hug and cuddle tight in love
To say a lot or little
As the mood was read
    But merely bye-bye dear he said.

THE LOSING GAME i

She walked into his heart
To stay a while
He loved her raven hair
And ready smile
Her movements were all quick
Like dancing flame
The joy he hoped to share
Just never came

He used to plan such tender things
His arms around
This soft smooth love of woman
That he'd found
But there are happenings
One can't explain
When joyful ecstasies of dream
Turn into pain

Though this he does admit
Is knowing life
The way it cuts through pleasures
Like a knife
Is something in one's destiny
We can't control
And all the joys and pain together
Make us whole

But what he cares for most
Is her content
To know that all her pains
Are freely spent
Is somehow satisfaction in itself
Within his life
For she, it seems, was never destined
As his wife.

Filton Hebbard

THE MAYPOLE OF LIFE

Sweet was the wind through the valley
Kissing the flowers that were wild
Taking me back through the ages
When I wandered there as a child
With dreams that can only be children's
Of love that flows over the world
Where life was a wonderful maypole
And colours and creeds were unfurled
But I sit now upon that green pasture
I pick a small flower from the ground
And I recollect pain that I've suffered
Until reaching the peace I've now found
But I think of how fine would the world be
If children had power to control
And the thoughts that they shared for tomorrow
Were the ones that revolved that maypole
Yes---- if the thoughts that they shared for tomorrow
Where the ones -----who revolved----- that------maypole.

THE PANACEA

They say Jack Spratt could eat no fat
His wife could eat no lean
Now what an exhibition
Their dinner must have been

To see Jack scratching at the fat
As he turned meat on a plate
Then scrutinising greasy bits
Pass them across to mate

And she in turn would ogle
At that congested oil
Her new false teeth on solid steak
Would never have to toil

Now if she put some butter in
And fluffed the mashed potato
Poor Jack would hug his stomach
Gall bladder cried no, no

And she if dining with a friend
Was forced to eat a chop
Knew that her poor intestines
All movement there would stop

But they did not die young in life
Regardless of their ails
They had within their bedroom
A balm when all else fails.

THE PEN AND ME AND YOU

I have waved my hand
    for ample reason
And no writing will it take
    out of season

I have measured my time
    the way I do
From a heart that beats
    like a heart that's true

Simple words are the ones I know
    as honest as the winds that blow
If gift I have it is to share
    with friends who are no longer there

And as the stars do twinkle down
    they take away that needless frown
For though my thoughts demand a page
    my pen is younger than my age

And you dear friends
    I'll always view
As the sun that shines
    down from the blue.

THE PHONE BOOK IS EMPTY

I've walked the long road
    for those many years
When I thought of you dear
    my eyes filled with tears

I've been ever lonely
    thinking of days
The days that were night-time
    for the writing of plays

I called it heaven
    with you in my arms
Whispering the small things
    that dressed you in charms

But now I must wonder
    since you've gone away
Have memories taught lessons
    that to you now say

You can't keep on looking
    for somebody new
For one day the mirror
    will bring truth to you

The truth that true loving
    is meant to remain
It's built on affection
    not a mixture of pain

Then that mirror will tell you
    that you've reached an age
When the phone book is empty
    as you turn a page.

Filton Hebbard

THE PILL

Once there was a little elf
Named Tickle – Him – Me – Too
He had so much of idle time
Much mischief did he do
He used to wander country lanes
Where lovers cuddled tight
To tickle them in places
So they wished that it was night

But he did get a certain shock
The time the hippies came
For they just got about it
Treating day and night the same
Though even if his mischief
Did make some girlies ill
He proudly claimed the reason
For production of the Pill.

THE QUEEN

The Queen, she stands, the way she sits,
    with utmost dignity
She is a symbol to admire,
    a face we long to see
She does not give herself a name,
    such as the Queen of Hearts
For she's the Queen of Royalty,
    the prestige of the Arts
She takes the blame in silence,
    for the deeds of other folk
When the troubled in their passion,
    so freely her revoke
She rides her cavalry of pain,
    through her dear London town
Where the millions stop to cheer her,
    from pleasure and renown
For even simple people,
    who work this saddened earth
Have hearts to help form judgement,
    on what true friends are worth.

Filton Hebbard

THE RACER

The hills rolled by with beauty
Bright sunshine tumbled down
Cars sparkled in great clusters
Like jewels upon a crown

The crowds were there in thousands
Massed at each vantage place
As they converged on Bathurst
To witness race on race

There was a gentleman aloof
A lesson to the lout
He focussed on a racer
This man he'd read about

They'd both known many summers
Since they'd been given life
And they were in their eventide
The Lord had claimed each wife

But with binoculars held firm
And close to his clear eye
He didn't know that very soon
A fine old gent would die

He envied much that racing man
A veteran through and through
As lean and hard and nerveless
He raced that car of blue

Grey clouds now lifted upwards
A sombre sky all dark
A fool upon his bugle played
The Last Post for a lark

And then our gentleman did see
The blue car swing and crash
The sight struck him quite motionless
As if he'd caught a lash

Then raising slowly up one hand
He bared his snow-white head
He knew without a telling
That a veteran was dead

But as he found his limousine
His eyes were not with sorrow
He knew that life was shortening
What future had the morrow

How truly lucky was a man
To reach three score and ten
Then die within his favourite sport
For fifty years his yen

And as that gentleman of ours
With care did drive away
He prayed to God to take him
As the racer went that day.

Filton Hebbard

THE TIME TO THINK

Set aside the time to think
    of what life seems to be

A struggle from the cradle
    to an unknown destiny

A day that's filled with laughter
    then a day that's filled with pain

A search beyond reality
    for a pasture blessed with grain

There is no endless comfort
    for a woman or a man

Unless they seek tomorrow
    as a catch me if you can

But when it comes to Christmas
    there's a day that stands alone

It is not a vague tomorrow
    it's a memory on a throne.

THE VILLAGE GREEN

I was sitting one day on the village green
For the nicest of sights were there to be seen
Then you came along
On your lips was a song
And the song that you sang was for me

But you didn't say yes
And you didn't say no
You rolled those big eyes
Should I come or I go
And the prettiest legs I did see

Then I stood to my feet with an offered arm
I longed for an image of gentleman's charm
With a curtsey and whirl
And a smile that was pearl
You bought heaven to earth just for me.

THE WAY IT GOES

Oh fool, oh fool, oh foolish man
You've worried since your life began
Why is that you act this way
As if the end comes every day

You worried of your grades at school
As though to fail would be a fool
And when you knew your looks were poor
What girl would ever cross your door

And with a most secure job
You thought that youth would surely rob
And you'd be out because of age
To seek positions page by page

And so your hair did slowly thin
There was no race that you could win
For they would call you baldy soon
With your long face like half a moon

Each time an ache took hold of you
Your sterling blood would turn to glue
Cancer moved from head to toe
As terrified to bed you'd go

Well if it weren't as bad as that
The Chinese meal was spiced with cat
No wonder you were pale and ill
Of that cat you had had your fill

Who swung that door – oh Agnes dear
What draughts can do to your left ear
And one day you'll an abscess get
What odds they'll simply call a vet

No one does love you very much
You're just a handy pocket touch
Those pains you get around your heart
Are far too bad for plain jam tart

Now how much money have you saved
A wooden box was all it paved
What cost was dying anyhow
Did savings banks that much allow

Good God you'd better save some more
On day you'll drop straight on the floor
Who said they close that pearly gate
You'd better hurry it's getting late

Imagine if you died in slumber
With half-done jobs of endless number
They'll never find that old trunk key
Or learn to prune the apple tree

And if they shouldn't find your will
Dear me a greater muddle still
But never mind and please don't fear
Your wife is quite a charming dear

She never worries very much
All your things she'll duly clutch
She'll make quite sure your coffin's paid
As stiff and straight you're in it laid

She'll even stroke your baldy head
To check that you are really dead
And after they have dropped you down
She'll go a-shopping on the town

She'll buy brief pants and a see-through bra
And the kids will sport a new Papa
He'll stretch out there before the fire
And puff awhile on your favourite briar

They'll kiss a bit and go to bed
While on that point enough is said
You've been a gent, a sort of toff
But brother, that's an awful cough.

Filton Hebbard

THE WILDERNESS OF LIFE

Within the wilderness of life
    there's much we never see

We move along a forward path
    that forms our destiny

We play our childhood games with zest
    and sometimes score a goal

But is it what is best for us
    in our specific role

For often near our eventide
    we stumble on a gift

Of something that lay in us
    but needed help to lift

And though we try to use it
    with thoughts of fellow man

The world has moved a chapter
    and we're an also ran.

THINGS WE USED TO DO

Do you recall those silly things we used to play and plan
When you would wear your mother's shoes and I would be a man
We'd hold our hands and giggle at romantic things
Like bands of grass that we would call our wedding rings
And with our school books we would build a home
With solemn vows that we would never roam
Do you recall

Do you recall the way we'd fingers-intertwine
And say the water fountain was our favourite wine
Then you would curtsy on a bended knee
And with your cheeky smile give a romantic plea
For time to vanish till we were both grown
And I could carry you across the threshold of our own
Do you recall

Do you recall that pain in later years
When life was bound to lose us in a flood of tears
The dreadful wrench of learning we must part
With no-one caring for those secrets of the heart
But as I hold you now with your return
The plans we made in childhood I still yearn
Do you recall

Do you recall
Why do I ask such foolish things
As our lips touch my heart so madly sings
Oh yes I know you do recall
And you remember all
That you recall.

Filton Hebbard

THOSE DREAMS THAT WE TOGETHER MADE

Walking alone in the darkness
Wondering where heaven could be
Feeling the pain of our parting
The reason why you should leave me

Thinking of plans that we cherished
Of the cottage that we would call home
With the children who played in the garden
And knowing that they were our own

Sweet Nelly I'll always remember
The way that you kissed in the night
Your body so warm and tender
As we cuddled ever so tight

But you were then taken to heaven
The place that some call paradise
I look to the sky and can't see it
The hereafter where everything's nice

Though why it should happen to you dear
Just why you were taken so soon
For our lives were at their beginning
As we made our plans 'neath the moon

And I am now left with my memories
The ones that I'll never let fade
For you were the heaven I dreamed of
In those dreams together we made

In those dreams that together we made.

TO EACH HIS OWN

Her legs were rather ugly
Curved outwards in their shape
Small children simply toddled through
And how the boys did gape

Her hair was lank and mousy
Her nose a shapeless knob
She was the plainest woman
The Lord's most careless job

She'd never had a boyfriend
Attended just one dance
To sit there like a wallflower
A figure in a trance

But she did have the finest heart
That one could hope to know
To lend and aid to a neighbour
Both day and night she'd go

Then one day she did nurse a man
Who'd fallen gravely ill
She'd taken him into her home
From where he'd lain so still

She relished tending over him
And lost him to her heart
He seemed as useless as a boy
Not knowing where to start

She knew he soon must leave her
Good health he'd gathered fast
She cried to think of parting
Not one rude word he'd cast

His eyes had never laughed at her
Through lens of deepest tint
Of money he was plentiful
And would not let her stint

Then one day he did draw her close
Sweet nurse you are so kind
Please help through my lonely life
For you must know I'm blind.

TO ONE AND ALL

He'd simply never known it to be that way before
There'd always been someone who'd knock upon his door

He'd never been lonely, he'd always had friends
To cuddle and kiss-up and make their amends

But to sit on a sofa and wait for the phone
That seemed to be broken and him all alone

Was something he'd always, scoffed at the chance
His life had been loving and filled with romance

So what was the reason why he felt that way
And the pillow beside him had nothing to say

Could there be an anguish that he'd tried to hide
For choosing a partner one had to decide

Does one seek out perfection or variety fair
And pass by a loved one who'd always be there

For life comes in chapters, just like a good book
And as one moves through it, it's prudent to look

Into a glass mirror where those secrets reveal
That the passage of time is an Achilles heel.

Filton Hebbard

TO SEEK A LOAN

The banker eyed across the room
His face as plain as porridge
This fellow thought there was a boom
He hadn't any knowledge
He'd asked for money – in a word
As if it grew on trees
Seemed as if he hadn't heard
There'd been a credit squeeze

The fellow twisted on his chair
He eyed that heavy door
No wonder bankers had no hair
Their worries came galore
Their questions flowed like mountain streams
Their eyes as big as chokoes
They rambled on for countless reams
Like doctors screening psychos

They'd set to business pretty fast
The chap did money need
His first word seemed to be his last
The banker had that greed
Collateral – kept bobbing out
It had St Vitus dance
His nerves it quickly put to rout
And dampness in his pants

That fellow was not destitute
He'd made that point quite clear
He wanted very little loot
To plant his granny dear
She'd up and died without a wink
Whilst drinking milk and honey
He'd never thought that on the brink
She'd cost a lot of money

The banker had the assets down
A house, a car, a boat
He'd written with a heavy frown
The children's nanny goat
Six lemon trees, a grapevine
A toy that gave a roar
The T.V set, the clothesline
Why did he ask for more

At last the fellow could endure
No further inquisition
His nature never was demure
Regardless of position
He blew his nose till it was red
His breath was coming hard
Keep your lousy dough he said
I'll plant Gran in the yard

The banker rose in all his charm
Good grief man, don't do that
You've assets longer than my arm
And Granny's no dead rat
Some eighty grand you show as wealth
Any you're my school pal, Morse
You also seem in perfect health
A hundred bucks – of course.

Filton Hebbard

TRY LOVING MY LOVE

Try smiling my friend
Your life is yours till its end
There'll be passion and pain
There'll be losses and gain
But that's life, that's life, my friend

Try laughing my sweet
Share fun with all you meet
There'll be tension and stress
There'll be much more than less
But that's life, that's life, my sweet

Try loving my love
Spend life with the partner you love
There'll be romance and joy
There'll be moods that annoy
But that's life, that's love, my love.

UNFORGIVING

I sit by my window
    I take in the view
But out of that window
    I'm looking for you
My mind keeps recalling
    the joy of your charms
As we lay together
    you close in my arms
They were tender moments
    that I'll never forget
Romance was our master
    the timing was set
But how could I know, dear
    that you'd walk away
I'd planned on a future
    where love came to stay
You offered no reason
    you fled with the dawn
Was I just a partner
    in passion or scorn
So now I must wonder
    for the rest of my life
Is there a true reason
    when a man takes a wife
Has he been a scapegoat
    or his partner a fool
For neither then could know
    if there is a rule
To learn the true meaning
    of words in the dark
Were they all sincere
    or part of a lark
And as I keep looking
    the scene grows so dim
In the cold light of morning
    am I somebody's whim
And I know that my loving
    will not be the same
I'll turn on my pillow

and know it's a game
I'll say all the sweet things
    that love wants to hear
Like forget all your troubles
    I'll always be near
But out in the sunshine
    I'll walk my own way
With a heart that is aching
    since you left me that day.

VULTURES

I saw that evil bird up high
    seeking out the next to die
It circled slowly round and round
    until a victim it had found
The morning air was fresh and clear
    and no-one knew that bird was near
But with its own majestic grace
    that vulture did its throne embrace
It knew that smaller birds were there
    and hunger would put them to air
So it would simply wait a while
    then feast the way that was its style
From lofty heights with bullet speed
    its claws would clutch to fill its need
And one sweet bird of handsome crest
    would never more return to rest
I wished there was a certain way
    that I could lift my voice and say
Stay safe within that lofty tree
    that evil bird will not get thee
He does his killing in full flight
    those leaves protect you from his might
But suddenly that small bird flew
    and for some moments lost my view
Though when it did return to sight
    those vicious claws held it so tight
And I could not but hate the world
    where such a doctrine passed unfurled
But suddenly I paused to think
    as clear as if with darkest ink
There resting at my dining place
    with sweetest smile on my wife's face
Baby lamb chops, my dear, she said
    and I found it hard to lift my head.

Filton Hebbard

WAR IS COMMON

Does any man of thinking
    feel he can prevent war
Or eliminate one raging
    beyond another shore

Literature is crowded
    where history records
On the fame of every nation
    with its gallant flashing swords

We pride our own athletic skills
    no matter what its type
And wave the banner of success
    with overbearing hype

We push across the mighty world
    from each and every side
That we most truly are the best
    that knowledge we'll not hide

We slide down snow-crest hilltops
    if that's where we were born
And view the tangled visitors
    with laughter dressed in scorn

We criticise the umpire
    when he penalises our man
For tripping an opponent
    and is ordered to the 'can'

So why do we think soldiers
    as fit as fit can be
Are not designed to muster
    for all the world to see

And show the trouble makers
    who push outside their walls
That they must take a backward step
    before the curtain falls

For every creature on the earth
    from strongest to the lame
Sets claim to certain privileges
    and knows it's not a game

And one might hold the upper hand
    for a measured length of time
But hidden by a beaten mask
    is an ever-growing lime.

Filton Hebbard

WE LIVE ALONE

All our lives are subject
    to the good things and the bad

And the joy in those around us
    softens lost ones who are sad

We are forced to bite and swallow
    life's common bitter pill

And the lady in the farmhouse
    knows that pain is never still

So if you seek a heaven
    to see in your back yard

Look first into a mirror
    to a heart that has grown hard

But if you see a kindness
    that is shared by one and all

The flowers that surround you
    will stand like poppies tall.

WHAT IS WEALTH

We search for wealth like beavers
To help us on our way
But is it truly wealth we need
For happiness to stay

Is it food we all are seeking
Or clothes, or cushioned bed
Or is it simple vanity
That plagues us till we're dead

Are we frightened of our future
Are we truly weak inside
We're proud of our achievements
But have we often lied

What is the real purpose
In reaching for the sky
When tensions steal affection
And love begins to die

My mind returns to childhood
In a rugged bushland home
Where everything was primitive
And hair saw little comb

We ran a mile or two to school
Sometimes without our shoes
For fitness had priority
To races we'd not lose

We'd often wear patched trousers
And raise an okay thumb
When the lady who repaired them
Was a tired, lovely mum

We had a single outing
It came each Saturday
If we had finished all our chores
It was a picture matinee

We'd organise a sandwich
Then through the bush we'd roam
To stumble on a mushroom patch
What joy to take them home

There were a host of pleasures
That didn't cost a cent
Like swimming in a farmer's dam
With compassion freely lent

So I look back oh so fondly
At the pleasures in real life
When any man could proudly boast
Of the cooking of his wife

When he didn't seek great fortunes
Or long trips overseas
And he loved the taste of billy tea
And toughened, natural cheese

When kids were never hungry
They ate what Mum set down
And Dad's only suit of navy blue
Was aired when he saw town

But I in my reflections
See wealth in many things
Like the wealth that flows in pleasure
From old-fashioned wedding rings.

WHO'S FOR THE DEVIL

So count your rosary beads
    or pray like hell
But don't like simple fellow think
    God answers every yell
Admit distressing crimes
    yes, freely those relate
Do not fulfil your promises
    though fill the outstretched plate
But brother you're as green
    as mighty steeples high
If you've the strangest notion
    that just before you die
You tell the Lord with fervour
    you really do lament
The hundred or one thousand times
    your black heart gave its vent
God has human knowledge
    of suffering and pains
His own Son took the message
    carried in his veins
So should you choose path crooked
    and in your crime you revel
No pleadings from your deathbed
    will save you from the Devil.

WORRY

As I lay there in darkness
In the small hours of the night
My thoughts went soaring from me
As if they were a kite

I felt the cushion 'neath my head
The comfort of deep foam
And yet my thoughts had left me
Why did they wish to roam

I'd worked so hard for many years
To gain myself a hold
On what folk call security
Before I grew too old

But as I gathered land and home
And other so-called wealth
I felt no anymore secure
For doubts crept in with stealth

I knew then that security
Was often split in twain
The lush green fields of pasture
Must wither without grain

There was so much to living
Not measured in a bank
And the joy of that security
Could easily turn rank

So when one takes security
And treats it as a word
There's money, health, society
Each one is worth a third

For if we gather money
And watch it pile up high
Can we feel quite secure
When school friends slowly die

And when we see the doctor
To have a routine check
He writes two words we can't discern
That look like human wreck

So when we think of all the things
We ever planned to do
The sands of time are running out
Am I as old as you

I worry then about my ails
And think of doctors fees
I see my money dwindle fast
And rest my shaking knees

With fading health and fortune
And less of social claim
The gap between my friends and I
Grew wider of its aim

There was a condescending air
A sort of..... 'poor old Jim'
Too bad he's lost the only things
That drew us close to him

The banker's nod was very curt
The gay-time crowd went by
As void of my security
Upon the bed I lie

I shake with painful knowledge
My hair is grey and thin
How could I lead the race so far
And in the end not win

I'd set aside my plans to roam
Till I'd secured my wealth
But now that I'd achieved it
It went with crippled health

I turned the pillow over
As I lay on the bed
The perspiration dampened it
My face was burning red

I knew then that I'd had a dream
That took me for a turn
Though sometimes dreams have value
If we from them do learn

For there's no real guarantee
That we will be secure
From fear of empty stomach
Or ails that have no cure

I'm not as old as in my dream
I'm healthy as can be
I'm not endowed with worldly wealth
Just eyes that clearly see

That there's no sure security
In this wide angry land
And I draw tight the bedclothes
With one, cold shaking hand

So I decide that with the dawn
I'll very earnest be
A man of simple happiness
Had that dream fooled poor me.

WORRY II

He was an intellectual
And she was rather dumb
He'd squirm at her stupidity
As she'd count from her thumb

She'd sit there every evening
As he'd expound a view
And she'd not pass opinion
Least he criticise her too

He said bread was a killer
Fermenting in the tubes
Though meat was of the nectar
Just swallow in large cubes

She rather liked sweet pastry
And ate it on the sly
She guessed it had no vitamins
But there's all ways to die

He saw her hips a-spreading
And gave a stern rebuke
You plump and foolish woman
Old age you'll never fluke

But he collapsed at forty nine
To fall down stony dead
And she his favourite cushion
Slipped underneath his head

She lived to eighty seven
And wondered what was right
Did pastry kill you quickest
Or worry in the night.

Filton Hebbard

YOUTH WILL HAVE ITS WAY

Walk softly through the garden
    where an old man you will find
And maybe he will let you stay
    awhile
Ask him for some knowledge of
    the years he's left behind
So you might blend the future
    to your style
He'll look at you with gentle eyes
    and lift a weary hand
Then indicate that you might
join him there
He'll tell you that all troubles
    are as free as running sand
And you'll have one for every
strand of hair
He'll laugh when he is saying
    that all hardships to a man
Are part of natures joy in
    being born
So don't think all the roses
    that surround him like a fan
Were not without the presence
    of a thorn
With tender words of wisdom
    he will make you understand
That pleasures are much
greater after pain
And if you have been dreaming
    of a mansion ever grand
Be happy with a roof that
    shelters rain
He'll look at you and
    wonder if there's any special thing
That he might know to help
you on your way
But warm within his pocket is
    a much-loved wedding ring
And he will wish you luck

and say goodbye
For all those years of living
    have taught him many things
But one thought rises high
above them all
No wisdom has good reason to a
    lover's heart that sings
And youth will go its way
    come rise or fall

Tommy

This story is fictional, illicitly a figment of imagination. But it could have been real.

It is intended to tell us that life and death are much deeper than their surface, that money is not happiness, that pain has no mercy, and that education has a lemon peel.

How often do these things happen in so many different ways?

Just who could claim to be educated? I mean educated.

The author.

It was one of those odd meetings that blossomed into love.

The office boy had returned with the luncheon sandwiches that had been ordered, and through his office window the executive saw the usual gathering of people in the city park. He'd often watched them as he'd eaten; all sorts; he'd thought them. Some were old men in their dark suits, walking as briskly as they could, for exercise he guessed, no food packages in their hands. Others were alone, looking for a place to squat, some male, some female. And the couples laughing together, holding hands, enjoying the sun shine; and if it were grey, the friendship, the togetherness.

But suddenly, on impulse, for no known reason, he lifted his package of sandwiches and decided to join them. He'd never done that before and for over two years he'd sat at his office desk and watched those luncheon people come, stay awhile, then go, to where? Back to their places of employment, he assumed.

He crossed the wide, busy street and passed through the open gate at the corner. Huge gates they were, swinging from their heavy, stone posts that shouldered the massive park fence like silent soldiers of war. They were open from sun-up to sun-down he'd noticed through-out the seasons when the pressure of business had kept him in the office for endless hours and returned him early.

Strangely, he felt like an intruder as if he shouldn't be there; so he looked for an inconspicuous seat, a place to sit and watch. He couldn't sit on the grass in his tailored, pin striped suit nor could he eat standing up. Gentlemen eating in public places must be seated his father had said. How often? Dozens of times. And his father had been poor.

In the distance, he saw a common garden seat beneath an over-hanging palm so he made towards it. Not in the sun, unfortunately, but with so many people choosing the carpet of lawn for their seating place he considered himself fortunate.

The seat was adequate for about four average adults and the young woman sitting there moved nearer to the distant edge without glancing up; it was a needless though instinctive courtesy move. He took the other edge and slowly ate his sandwiches, wondering as he did so, whether or not he ought to offer her something.

She was reading a dark, leather bound book and seemed engrossed in it, so he made a point of looking away as he ate. He enjoyed taking in the scene, and quietly wondering about all the people who were walking, talking, laughing, and generally appreciating the life around them.

After awhile, the young woman closed her book, slipped it into a small raffia shopping bag, murmured a quiet 'pardon me' for reasons unknown, and headed towards the entry gates and disappeared from sight.

She was beautiful; good figure, nice facial features, glossy dark hair, and smartly dressed.

Back in the office, she kept returning to his mind. He wondered why she had chosen that dark, sunless, and perhaps unfriendly seat! What was she reading in that deeply engrossed manner? Where did she work? What was her vocation?

He cursed himself. He had work to do and she was disturbing his concentration and that was as foolish as his reason for taking his lunch into the park in the first place. And they hadn't spoken. Well she had, 'Pardon me', she'd said as she'd left.

The following day was as sunny as the day before and when he ordered his sandwiches, he added, 'and two of those large lamington cakes that they have in the canteen.'

The office boy looked surprised. "Two Sir. But you never eat cakes."

He smiled. "I will today."

And the office boy was right; he didn't eat any cake that day, he gave the lamingtons to passing children.

With a quickening heart and a lightened step, he had left the office and dodged the traffic, to reach, and pass through that ominous gateway; strange, anxious thoughts in his mind. He asked himself. Was he going stupid, childish?

Casually, glancing from side to side, he strolled down the pathway between the lawns until he was near to the park bench of yesterday, nestling beneath the overhanging palm.

The seat was vacant. Damn. It was true; he was acting childishly. So he ate his sandwiches, gave his cakes to passing children and returned to the office. What did he care about that young woman? He didn't know her; he hadn't even spoken to her. He was a 'nut case', that's what he was, a proper nut case. She might have been a tourist from another state; from anywhere at all, never to return.

And what would he have said if she had been there. Nothing probably, plain nothing. And the cakes, what would he have done with those! A grown man offering a woman he'd never met a cake. Hell his face burnt.

'Would you like a lamington Madam? It's fresh. The canteen gets them in fresh every morning'. Hell childish.

Back in his office, he stared through the window at the scene across the park. It was beautiful in the sun-shine, but quieter now that the majority of the public were seated in some form or other. He hadn't stayed for the full period of his luncheon break. But then his skin tingled.

The cup of tea he'd made in his small privileged closet shook in his hand. A cold warmth ran through him. She was there; he could see her; she was looking at the people as she walked along the meandering pathway.

The urge to leave his office and return to the park was tearing at him but he sat fixed of eye until she disappeared from view; and he knew, he was positive, she had taken a seat on that same park bench.

He continued to sit, staring through the window, until, as the lunch hour closed, there was general movement towards those powerful entry gates. She was among them, walking slowly still looking about, and he stood to place his head against the window to gain the last glance of her before she disappeared from view.

The next morning, rain fell. He cursed it, yes, it was good for the lawns and the country farmers and the reservoirs, but he still cursed it.

And the office boy smiled as he looked in to take the order.

"Two more lamingtons, Sir, You must like them,"

'I thought everybody liked lamingtons."

"I guess so, Sir. My mother makes real beauties. She dips them deep into that liquid chocolate stuff before she rolls them in the coconut. Sometimes it soaks halfway through."

It was easy to return his smile. "She knows you'd love that."

There was a youthful laugh, "She eats a lot of them herself."

But light rain was falling when the luncheon break fell due and although a few of the 'hardy' defiant lovers passed through that proud and dominant gateway of the park, he ate his sandwiches alone in the office.

The two lamingtons were in a separate bag. He looked at that brown paper bag containing the cakes, slipped into his coat that he'd hung in a small recessed wardrobe that indicated the elevated significance of his office, grasped his wide, black umbrella that lurched in one corner, and made his way out to the street, before crossing to the park entrance.

A few spots of fine rain touched his face, so he unfolded the umbrella and entered the park, wondering as he did so why he was behaving so out of character. He liked rain, even enjoyed walking in it with the carefree clothing of recreation time, but not in the prim and proper house of employment. They had a name for him in the business world, and although they never used it to his face a friend had passed it on. He didn't mind, he was proud of it.

"They call you Mister Right", his friend had said. "You dress properly, you speak properly, and what you say is what you mean. It's one of the reasons for your success. You never go back on your word."

He walked slowly down the sealed pathway, noticing the vacant lawns that had lost their attraction to the damp, and the few who had moved to the dubious shelter of trees, not quite knowing why he was there; before he paused, disbelieving.

Beneath the palm, sitting alone was the young lady with whom he had shared that park bench two days earlier. He hadn't seen her arrival even though he felt certain that his sight had been captivated by that ominous park gate-way for every moment of his luncheon interval.

He hesitated, them walked across the spongy, wet lawn to take his place at the far end of the bench. Would she stand to her feet and leave, suspecting him of an ulteria motive! She was reading the same book, seemingly not noticing him. He sat the bag containing the lamingtons to one side and drew the umbrella to the centre of his legs with intent to close it.

"Move it up," she murmured softly, "We could share it. The tree leaks."

His hands shook with her words. Was he a school boy or was he really an executive of a robust commercial enterprise. "I... I... we could both shift a bit," he suggested, "so different to yesterday." Her book, he then saw, was the Bible.

"Yesterday," she repeated, "I'm sorry about that, I came late."

Should he pinch himself? Was this a dream? "I came over" he said. "I work across the street. I thought if you were here we could talk about something."

"Such as?" She had moved to share the shelter of the umbrella.

"Anything at all. Nothing special. It's silly, I know, but when I saw you reading such an important looking book I knew we must have something in common. Young people don't seem to read much nowadays."

"I'm twenty eight."

He gave a brief laugh. "That's young; I'll be forty in a couple of years."

"Forty is still young; life begins at forty my father used to say." She smiled. "Are you married?"

"No."

"Why not? You're handsome and look as if you have a good job."

"Thank you for the first part but your right about the job. I'm well paid."

"Aren't there any girls where you work?"

He laughed. "Only about thirty."

"And you haven't found one to love?"

He felt the paper bag rattle in his hand and it provided a diversion.

"I've got a couple of lamingtons here, you know, those cakes. Would you eat one?"

"Yes. I love them." She extracted a cake from the bag and bit a piece from it. He took the other.

"You haven't answered," she said.

"What?"

"About finding a girl to love – at work."

He paused, as if he preferred not to answer. "You're very assertive," he replied. "We're talking like old friends and we've only just met."

"I know. But why should two people tiptoe around when they are both awake. You were looking for me before you sat here, weren't you? Today I mean."

"Yes. And you were looking for me yesterday when you came late. I was looking out through my office window."

"Yes. I was looking for you. I wasn't sure why but that is the reason for me being late yesterday."

"I don't quite follow you."

"I'll tell you after you answer my question."

"What question?"

"About thirty girls at work and not a single one to love."

"It hasn't been like that. As a child I never had much. We were poor. I wanted a different life for my wife and family. I had to succeed."

She nodded understandingly eating a little more of her cake and dusting coconut crumbs from the lap of her dress. "But you're successful now, I can tell by your appearance and the way you speak."

"I suppose so, though they aren't my type. The office girls."

"What! Not one out of thirty?"

"I say good morning to them and good afternoon when they leave. I don't have anything in common with them. I never talk about life."

"You're talking about life with me."

"You're different?"

"In what way?"

"I don't know. I sat on this seat two days ago. You were here before me. We didn't converse in any form and yet I kept thinking about you for the rest of that day and all of the next. Yesterday, I bought two lamingtons and gave them to some kids."

"Like today. One for me?"

"Stupid, wasn't it?"

"No. That's why I was late yesterday."

"Like I said, I don't follow you on that point."

"I had to call in at the church. I had to talk to God.... about you."

He stared at her; her hazel eyes gleaming with intelligence, the whites clear. "Am I supposed to laugh," he asked, not fully comprehending her remark.

"You don't believe me," she stated.

"It isn't that I don't believe you. I simply can't see why you would go to church in the middle of the day for any reason, let alone to talk about a man you'd never met."

"I had met you; I met you two days ago. Remember?"

"But we didn't speak."

"Not with words, with intuition. It flowed between us, didn't it? We both admitted to looking for each other yesterday. Why?"

"I don't know," he stated simply.

"I do," she responded. "We met through God. He guided our thoughts."

He wished he could tell her that she was talking nonsense but the words wouldn't form. She was explaining her thoughts and he knew that he couldn't explain his own. "And what did God tell you?" He asked suppressing the urge for cynicism.

"You don't believe in God, do you?"

"Nor Santa Clause nor Easter Bunny."

"God doesn't tell you anything. God instructs our minds, then leaves it to us to decide which direction we should take."

He ate the remainder of his lamington before speaking. "I must admit. Help from any direction can be appreciated when the pressure's on. Even from Santa Clause."

"Do you have a religion?"

"No."

"Why not? What went wrong?"

"I don't think anything went wrong. We weren't a church – going family. My parents never said why. No money to spare for the plate maybe. I grew up thinking I had a religion until I was old enough to realize that I knew absolutely nothing about that religion. And when I say nothing, I mean nothing."

"That's sad."

"I don't feel sad. It's something I don't have to bother about. Perhaps I'm lucky."

She shook her head. "You aren't lucky."

"I've got a well paid job, I own a cottage, I have a superannuation policy and a reasonable amount in a Bank. Isn't that being lucky at thirty eight years of age."

"You don't have a wife and family."

"True." He looked into her eyes; and jocularity in his voice faded. "That's where I'm not lucky. I'd love to have a son. A daughter would be fine, of course, but I'd like to give my son the things that I wanted as a child and could never have. If I had a daughter my wife could give her the things that girls would like to receive when they're young. I don't know what girls long for and maybe never receive."

"Love, girls long for love."

"Well, they all get that."

"How do you mean?"

"Sex is love, isn't it?"

"No. When they're young girls yearn for sex and think its love. It isn't. Sex is sex, love is love, God is God......."

"And I'm an atheist." He intruded into her line of speech; but they both smiled.

"Who wants a son," she added.

"Yes."

"I'll give you a son," she stated unhesitatingly.

Breath held in his lungs. He was nonplussed. What did she mean? What was that she'd said earlier........ no point in tip toeing when you're both awake? Some-thing like that. "I mean a boy of my own," he uttered.

"So do I," she confirmed.

"You mean.......marry?"

"Yes."

"But our first conversation stated half an hour ago. We don't know each other."

"Yesterday when I went to the church I asked God for guidance. I said that I'd sat next to a man to whom I'd never spoken and yet I feel that I'd known him for all of my life."

Strangely, he knew that he felt the same. He could talk to the woman about nothing, anything, every thing. "And you received a message or something. "He said.

"I received an understanding, a confirmation of my thoughts. God doesn't speak to people with words. I told you that. He simply fills you with the right to decide."

"But I told you something, too. I don't believe in God. You do. How could we marry in a church?"

"We wouldn't need to. Churches are a communication point, a place to express your faith. The law is the registry office."

He dragged the palm of his free hand over his face, his other hand still grasping the shaft of his umbrella. He knew that he wanted what he had just heard and yet it had arrived too quickly to be accepted or appreciated. Or had it? He did feel as if he'd known her for all of his life....... and he did want a son to call his own.... to walk with, to run with, to play with; to teach about life, to read to, to give things that his own childhood had missed. "We might have a daughter." he said suddenly as if he agreed with the general proposition. "I'd love a daughter, too, very much. But I was a boy, you see, I know what boys need, what they want."

"I would ask God for a boy."

"Oh, hell, not that stuff again."

"If I ask God for a boy you would have a son. I know, I know, I know. If you believe nothing else, please believe what I have just said."

"Are your feelings on religion that strong?"

"I have no faith in religion, as religion goes. Religion is a slaughter house. I read the other day that there were nearly four hundred different religions in America."

"Not correct, I suppose, but it was in a magazine."

"What then?"

"My faith is in God, not religion."

"I know I could love you," he said. "It's screaming at me. But let us talk some more. Tomorrow? Here?"

"Yes. We'd better get back."

They both stood, she kissed his cheek. "Tomorrow," she said. "Is that a promise?"

"I never break a promise."

She kissed him again. "And what will we call our son?"

He gave an embarrassed laugh. "I... I Tommy. My father's name was Thomas. He was a good man."

"Then Tommy it is. He will be a good Christian."

"Do we have to bring that into it."

"It will be good for him. He will need it."

Two months later they married in a register office.

It was a gala event; the most eligible bachelor in the firm. The heir-apparent to the position of General Manager, had married. The staff crowded the sweeping Board room and expressed their best wishes; the incumbent chairman eulogised on the service given and the future to behold.

She stunned them with her beauty, her charm, her self assurance.

"Family. What did they plan? One child, two, three or four? Was she already on the way?"

"No. We'll do it proper. Three months before I conceive. And it will be a boy, a son for my husband."

"And later?"

"A daughter for both of us."

"After that?"

"Who knows."

"Are you sure it will be a son first?"

"Yes. I have spoken to God." laughter, then:

"Who goes to church? Sunday is for football."

"I go to church every Sunday and sometimes mid-week."

More laughter. They all knew his atheistic views.

"Will he go with you?"

"I doubt it."

Laughter again. Hell, she was funny. Church mid-week. She was a scream. Even priests and parsons didn't go to church mid-week. Did they? Someone better tell her that churches didn't open during the week. Sunday was collection day, Or was that right? In the cinemas the churches seemed to be open all of the time. But how could you believe what you saw in a cinema? Make believe, that's all. They ought to make those American pictures give the proper trading times for churches.

And so the banter continued until they departed on their honeymoon. And for awhile after, no doubt.

At the doorway, the chairman kissed her cheek, gently and seriously wishing her good luck for the birth of a son. "You have a good man," he added.

"With the will of God" she'd replied. "And I love my husband."

Actually, they didn't journey away on their honeymoon; they stayed in the cottage that he'd purchased many years before.

"There are signs of "Men Only" in every room." She'd said with a laugh when he'd first introduced her to it. "It needs a new broom."

"Then I'll buy a new broom."

She'd hugged him. "I am the new broom and I have special plans for this son of ours."

"You're sure of yourself, aren't you?"

She'd shaken her head. "No. It isn't myself that I'm sure of."

He didn't push it further, there was work to be done.

The cottage wasn't large but it was comfortable. Situated in a leafy street in a good suburb it blended nicely with the surrounds, and was void of ostentation.

"We could sell it and buy something bigger and better," he suggested. "I'm on a handsome salary."

"Bigger and better," she'd facetiously mocked. "You, the boy who bathed in a washing tub before the kitchen fire."

"I shouldn't have told you that. I'll never live it down."

She'd kissed him. "I'll square it off for you. I stood in a dish and did the whole job with a face cloth."

He'd laughed audibly. "Hell. I'd love to have seen it. Until what age?"

"About ten or eleven."

"Where was the rest of the family?"

"Mum chose the times. But that's why our son will have a lovely room of his own. A desk of his own for his studying, heated for the winter, air-conditioning for the summer, the works. I want him to love his life here and be ready for the hereafter when his time has come."

Talking about the hereafter!!! She wasn't even pregnant. He hesitated.

"I'll put the kettle on," he said, moving to the kitchen. He wished she didn't toss in the religious bits every now and again, but did it matter she never expected him to take her to church nor even drive her there. She rattled off in her own little V.W.

Her thoughts were hers, his thought's were his.

He'd taken a month's leave and there was plenty to do in it; the usual things, wallpaper, paint, carpets new furniture. A total inside facelift.

And outside; lawns revamped, flower beds, resurfacing the paths, even a double seated garden swing.

"I'll sit next to young Tommy," she said as she moved gently back and forth on the stiff, board seat.

Satisfied after three weeks of effort, they photographed their achievements and spent the next week appreciating the atmosphere before returning to employment.

"I'll carry on until Tommy gets too heavy," she said with a smile, and three months later, true to her announcement at the wedding celebration's she stated over the evening dinner. "I'm six days over with my 'mens' so Tommy's on his way."

He was delighted, leaving his seat to kiss her on all the flesh spot's he could see, until she giggled and pushed him away.

"Wait until we've washed the dishes." she said. "Then you can start again if you wish."

Which he did. He was elated, a child of his own. Wonderful. The boy could be anything he chooses soon as he was old enough to make sensible decisions. Engineering maybe, or law, or medicine, or dentistry or design. Boat design .. there was good money in that.

He collected his thoughts. He was thinking foolish. Children had to be born first, and secondly, they had a right to make their own choices. And thirdly, most importantly, it might be a girl after all.

"It'll be a boy," she said. "I know, I've been told."

He changed the subject. She was beautiful in every way. He loved her.

And the next eight months were ecstasy. More plans, laughter, shopping, tummy touches, giggles in the mirror, just wonderful.

And Tommy was born.

The message came through to his office. "Your wife has been taken to the hospital."

Thirty seconds later he was out on the footpath waving for a taxi.

At the hospital, before he found the correct ward, he stopped a passing nurse, she smiled at his anxiety.

"Ward twenty three," she said, "but if you want to see him first, just look through that glass panel. He's in there."

"She's had it already?"

A laugh. Then, "Yes. I nearly had to catch it."

"And it's a boy."

"It's a boy, a beautiful boy."

He looked through the glass as instructed. There were five babies on display. The name was at the head of the cot. Tommy.

He ran back to the nurse. "Has he got all of his toes and everything?"

"I told you. He's a beautiful boy."

He was peering through the glass pane again. Tommy yawned. He waved. He's smiling at me, he thought. He knows I'm his father."

He forced himself away and found Ward 23. It was directly behind the glass panel, but he found it.

She was there; a bit pale but looking good. He hugged her. She laughed at his obvious, uncontrolled excitement.

"I've seen him," he said. "I waved at him and he smiled."

She laughed. "I thought you were going to say he waved back. After all he is about thirty minutes old."

"And you. How are you?"

"Pretty good, glad it's over."

"Did it hurt?"

"Not as much as the pleasure it gave."

"I love you."

"I love you, too."

"I think I'll learn tap dancing."

She laughed again, reaching up with opened arms to pull him down towards her. "I told you, didn't I?"

"Told me what?"

"That it would be a boy."

"You're clever," he said. "That's why I asked you to marry me."

"It was my idea, wasn't it?"

"Well. I said you're clever."

And the rest of that year, and the next, was heaven.

Tommy had inherited the beautiful smile of his mother; it lit his face like the sun the sky. When his father returned from work each day and looked down into the boy's cot, the smile of recognition was a father's paradise.

"He knows I'm his Dad. He can tell already and he can't talk."

251

"He knows you love him. That's what he knows. And rightly so. The only father who could care more than you is the Father of all of us."

He laughed and lifted Tommy from the cot to cradle him in his arms. The banter that often passed between them on religious or unreligious themes was never an offence. They had adapted a painless he – thinks she – thinks approach to life. "What do you make of that Tommy," he said as the child tried to put a finger in his father's eye, "your mother believes Fairy Tales."

"Take no notice if him, Tommy," she responded with a smile. "I think he failed at school."

"Top of the class, Tommy, that's what I was. And you'll be the same."

And so it was between them. She never asked him to join her unfailing attendance at Sunday church service, and he never offered to go.

"I can't pray for anything," he said on one occasion, "no matter what it is. I'd feel such a fool. And as far as thanking somebody I've never seen for my daily bread when I work hard for my monthly pay cheque, would be ridiculous. I work for a large firm. That firm provides my daily bread."

"And don't forget how you got your job."

"How do you think I got it?"

"You told me. You were invited by a stranger."

"He's not a stranger now. He kissed your cheek at that reception after we married."

"Yes. He wore an expensive aftershave, too. But he was a stranger when he rang to offer you the position you hold. Why did he do that?"

"That's cheating," he argued with a laugh. "Everybody knows "I'm brilliant. That's why Tommy smiles at me. He knows he's got a smart father."

He doesn't know you're his father. And you're dodging the subject."

"What subject?"

"Why you were invited to your job."

"Word of mouth. That's what it was."

"Do you want to know something?"

"Of course I want to know something. Anything you're got to offer."

"Your boss goes to the same church as me."

"Hell. I didn't know that." He was clearly surprised. "You're seen him there?"

"I talk to him. Every Sunday."

"Well, I'll be buggered." It's a wonder he employed me. I make no bones about my thoughts. Especially religion."

"I married you and I make no bones about my thoughts either."

"That's different. You were after sex."

"I wasn't after sex. I was after you and so was the manager of your firm. He sat near to you at a Dinner somewhere. He said he sensed that you were a person he wanted."

"Like you."

"Yes. Like me. There was a vacancy in his firm and he knew you were the man for it."

"He told you that? After church?"

"Yes."

"But I knew nothing about the nature of his firm. Not then. I picked it up."

"Why do you think he made contact with you?"

"I don't know. I've often wondered."

"Think, man, think."

"Oh, come on. Not the mystic art of the unknown world."

"Of course not. And I'm not talking voodoo. Something guides the way people act. Can't you see that?"

"Yes. But that's the way they are."

"There's more to it than that," she said. "What about intuition. It's like memory. You can't pick it up and look at either of them. But they are still part of you."

"What does that mean, in your language?"

"It means that everybody could have a soul. An invisible part of us that doesn't die when our flesh dies."

"I'd bet a dollar that our memory dies when we're dead."

"Not if your soul took you to heaven. Heaven is where people all meet again. It wouldn't be much good unless we remembered each other."

"My heaven is at the dinner table each night, with you at one end, Tommy sitting beside me in his high chair, and a plate of your top class cooking before me."

"I think you'd better take Tommy for a walk in his stroller before your heaven comes to a sudden end."

He kissed her. "You're beautiful, I love you. I even love your upside down thinking." He sat Tommy in his stroller and buckled him safely. "What do you make of your mother, Tommy?"

"Gah." Tommy replied with one of his beautiful smiles. "Gah."

They disappeared through the doorway.

At the age of three Tommy attended church for the first time. By then, he didn't cry without a good reason, and he could speak and listen at appropriate comments.

His father hated to see him leave the house with his mother; not because of the venture into the world of religion, about which he would know nothing for a few more years, but because Sunday was 'Dad's Day.' It was losing the boy's company for those two hours; it was the sharing of laughter, of together on the back yard swing, of tumbles on the lawn, and the partnership of family love.

"You come, Daddy," the boy would say as, he and his mother prepared to leave, on almost beseeching tone in his voice.

"No, Tommy. I have to get ready for when you come home. We've got lots of things to do together."

"You not go nowhere, Daddy."

"No, Tommy. You be nice and quiet in the church, and when you home we'll do games together. Your mummy will take good care of you."

And almost stumbling as he walked to the little car, holding his mother's hand but constantly looking backwards, Tommy would stand on the seat waving until he was out of sight.

And always, never failing, his father's eyes would mist with emotion.

"I'll miss that boy so much when I've gone, sweet heart," he one day said to his wife.

She'd looked sharply at him with concern. "You aren't sick are you? Something you're hiding from me, Dear God I don't want to lose you."

He'd brightened and hugged her, "No, no, no problems. It's silly, I know, but I am over forty now, and every day is one day nearer."

"Forty. Heavens. That's half a man's age nowadays. You mustn't think silly. It's not like you."

"Well, I've never had a son before I simply didn't know how much it could mean to a father."

"And a mother."

"Of course, I'm sorry."

"You gave me a fright. Men are so hopeless sometimes. They try to act tough and they aren't tough at all. Frightened of doctors, lots of them. My father was one. Had prostrate problems. Running to the toilet three or four or five times a night. Saying that everybody's got a weak bladder as they get older. But it was cancer, damn it. And he left it too late."

"Well, I don't run to the toilet during the night. You know that. I'm well. I'm fit, I'm a rubber ball."

"Yes. A rubber ball at forty who probably won't die before his baby boy turns forty. He'll probably have a family of his own by then."

"Okay. I'm silly. You said I'm silly and I'll agree. But I'll tell you something. I had a dream the other night and I was dead. I was looking at myself and I was dead. I was starring down at myself and I said. "Yes, that's me. I know the shirt. It was a birthday present from my wife."

She laughed, jerkily. "You recognised yourself by looking at a shirt?"

"Yes. It seemed real. Very real. I was damn pleased to awaken and see you beside me."

"You're crazy."

"I think you'd better have another baby."

"I can't. I can't conceive again."

"What do you mean?"

"Just that."

"Just what?"

"I can't conceive. I've been to the doctor about it and had tests."

"Hell. No mate for Tommy!"

"You're his mate. He wouldn't want anybody else. You know what he does in church?"

"How could I. I'm not there."

"He keeps looking at the doorway. For you. He doesn't say anything but you know how he is after we return home. He runs to get to you. He loves you."

"Not as much as I love him."

"And I love you both so let's not talk about being apart. I don't want to ever think about it."

"But about a second child. We can talk about that."

"No. It's out of bounds."

"It could be me, you know."

"You! You're a rubber ball, remember?"

"Ample sperm doesn't mean anything for certain. I'll have some tests."

"You don't need tests."

"What is that supposed to mean?"

"It means that it wouldn't matter what the results of a test indicated."

"Now that's silly. But I'm the silly one, I've admitted it. Your tests must have shown – up poorly."

"No. I'm okay."

"Then it's me."

"No. She pressed close to him and his arms automatically embraced her. She could not fail to see his concern. "You won't like what I have to say."

"I like everything you say even when you talk about Mister Spook."

"That's what it is."

"Not religion."

"Well. In a way. When I was in hospital after having Tommy, I had a visitor."

"Yes, me. And lots of others."

"When I was asleep. It was in a dream, I think. I don't know for certain. I thought I was awake when it happened."

255

"What happened?"

"I heard a voice even though I couldn't see anybody."

"If you heard a voice you had to be awake."

"I didn't see anybody. But the next morning I thought I must have dreamt it."

"What was it?"

"The voice told me that I wouldn't have any more children."

"Forget it. It was a dopey dream. Like mine when I saw myself dead."

"That's not the way I felt it."

He pushed her away until he could hold her by the shoulders and look into her eyes. "It's me," he said. "I must have become infertile. I'll see the quack."

"I don't think so. See your doctor if you want to. But I have a funny feeling about it."

"Oh, come on. I saw myself dead and I'm not dead. We think of things that happen to other people and we worry about the same things happening to ourselves...... then we have rotten dreams. I'll see the doctor and I'll bet he puts me on to hormones."

"Sure, you do that," she said, but her voice was flat.

Tommy entered the room to close the conversation. "Mummy and I are going to have a piece of cake, Tommy, would you like some."

"Yes, please, Daddy, a big piece."

A week later, he spoke to his wife during an interval in the television program. Tommy was asleep in his room. "The doctor rang me about my sperm count test."

"And."

"He reckons they're fighting each other to be the first one out the door."

"So there's no reason why I don't fall pregnant."

"Yes," he admitted slowly. "There's something wrong somewhere."

"There's that old saying."

"Which one. There are heaps of old sayings."

"God works in mysterious ways."

"Not that again. Please. God is an expression. It simply means the world in which we live. The sun, the flowers, the trees."

"Yes. And to whom do we owe our thanks?"

"For the world?"

"Yes."

"I don't know. Nobody knows. But I do know that a single spook didn't shovel it all together."

"God isn't a spook .... as you call it."

"No. He's the master of hide and seek."

"You're half right. The seek part. Seek and you shall find."

"I was seeking coffee this morning and I didn't find any."

"We'd run out. There's a new packet there now?"

"Good. I'll make some. Should I make a third cup in case we have a visitor?"

"Yes. I think I need two. The spare one's to throw over you before it gets cold."

"So now I know. You want to warm me up. You're after sex again."

He kissed her quickly before she could respond.

Their lips parted and she managed. "You're the one who's always after sex."

"And coffee."

He struggled out of the lounge. "I'll make some tea."

"You said coffee."

"For the guest."

Tommy entered the room, rubbing the backs of his hands across his eyes. "Daddy?"

"Yes, Tommy. You should be asleep."

"It's dark, Daddy."

"I'll turn the light on and read to you and stay until you go to sleep again."

"And leave wite on. I don't like dark, Daddy." The boy's eyes filled with tears.

With a glance of concern towards his wife, he lifted the boy into his arms. "What is it, Tommy? What don't you like?"

"I get flitend in the dark, Daddy, when you gone."

"But I'm in the room next to you, with Mummy. The dark won't hurt you. It helps us go to sleep."

Tommy shook his head. "Dark not nice. I can't see nuffing." There was fear in his tone.

"If you call out, I'll come. I always do that. You know I'll come."

Tommy shook his head again, stretching to wrap his arms around his father's neck. "Please don't leave me in dark, Daddy."

"I'll never leave you anywhere, Tommy. If Mummy isn't with you, I'll be there."

The boy gave his beautiful smile, and when his father lowered him to the floor he ran to his mother. "Good Daddy, Mummy."

They hugged each other, a strange fear in her own mind. There was something somewhere that she should remember. "Yes, Tommy your Daddy is a good Daddy. He'll take care of you when it's dark. And we'll both take care of you when it's light."

"When God turn sun on."

The boy's father stared, at the boy, then at his wife.

"Yes," she answered, catching her husband's expression. "Now Daddy will put you to bed again."

"Wif wite on?"

"Yes with Daddy's light on because it's night time."

So the boy's father tucked him into bed again, read a child's bedtime story until the little eyes closed, stood on a chair to soften the ceiling light with a napkin, and returned to the lounge room. "You aren't stuffing that God's light into him already, are you?"

She shook her head. "No. I never say a word about religion. Something must have been said about God's light in one of the sermons. I don't remember anything in particular."

But the next day, the boy's father purchased a bedside lamp that effused a soft un-disturbing glow, and to please his wife, he chose one in the shape of an angel.

Tommy was delighted; "Like on windows where I go wif Mummy," he said.

"Yes, Tommy, it's like an angel." As the words slipped out, he knew it was a mistake.

"What's an angel, Daddy?"

He looked at his wife. She had joined him to see the boy's reaction to the lamp. Her face was expressionless, and he had been adamant on more than one occasion. "Never tell the child a lie," he had said. "They believe everything their parents say, they have no choice. Parents are their early tutors."

"Mummy knows angels better then me, Tommy. She'll tell you."

"No, Daddy, you gave me angel."

He looked at his wife again and she sensed his agony. Her lips opened but he shook his head. He had created his own problem.

"That is not an angel, Tommy. It is a lamp, a lamp that looks like an angel because it has light in it."

"Do angels have wite in dem?"

Hell. How does a father explain something to a four year old boy when he doesn't believe what he was obliged to say?

"There are all sorts of lights, Tommy. We turn a little switch on and the globe up there puts light into a room. That's called electric light. When you were a baby I picked you up and said you were light, but now that you're a big boy I say you are heavy. Light means easy to lift up and heavy means hard to lift up. When you draw with your colour pencils and you make some of the sky with your blue pencil you make a light sky and when you draw a cloud with rain in it with your black pencil you make a dark sky."

"I don't like dark, Daddy. I tole you. I tole you."

"I know, Tommy, that's why I brought you the little lamp to make a light for you even through the night time."

"The angel light."

"Yes."

"You not tell me what angel light was, Daddy."

He glanced at his wife again and she saw his indecision. He wouldn't lie, he didn't know the truth, but he had to say something.

She spoke for him. "Angel light is light we can't see, Tommy," she tried to explain, her voice husky with the emotion of confusion and the awareness of her husband's blunt philosophy concerning religion. "It's not real light like out in the sunshine. It's like.... you know when you hear Daddy come home and run to the door to meet him."

Tommy nodded.

"You have that lovely smile of yours and your eyes are shining because you're happy to see Daddy again..... and I say to myself Tommy has the light of an angel on his face."

Tommy seemed as if he were trying to unfathom his mother's words. "Am I angel, too, Mummy?"

"Yes, Tommy, you are an angel we can see." she hugged him.

"Are there wots of sorts of angels, Mummie?"

"Yes, Tommy, lots of different kinds."

He looked at the bedside lamp. "And that's a girl one."

"It's what a girl angel would look like if we could see her."

Tommy looked at the bedside lamp again."

"Do dey have dark angels, Mummy?"

"No, Tommy, only ones that give light. There are no bad angels; they are all nice, and all good."

"Thanks, Mummy; I get flitend when it's dark. I told Daddy."

"Well, it won't be dark anymore. Daddy's little angel lamp will give you light all through the night time."

He smiled. "And in day time I'll have God's sun."

"Yes," his mother replied, glancing at her husband.

"Kiss me, Mummy."

She kissed him.

"Will you read me a story, Daddy?"

"Yes. Tommy. I'll read you a story."

And that was a wonderful era in their lives.

Saturdays were shopping in the morning and down the beach in the afternoon if it were sunny, or games inside if it were bleak.

Sundays were church for Tommy and his mother after dressing in their newest clothes and Tommy throwing kisses from his fingertips as they departed in the morning; and games on the lawn with his father in the afternoons if it were sunny, and the reading of children's stories if outside weather were unkind.

They made good memories.

And Tommy loved his bedside angel lamp. He called it "Mary" after a kind little girl in one of the stories his father read to him. Mary always saved some of her evening meal to give to stray animals that regularly seemed to be passing her door at the right time.

"Mary a nice angel," Tommy often said in a determined tone as he switched on his bedside lamp. "She keeps nasty dark away."

"All angels are nice, Tommy. You have to be a nice boy and you are my angel."

"Not proper angel like the lightie."

"No, Tommy," his mother agreed. "But the light isn't a proper angel, either. Not really. The light is a make believe angel. It tells us what angels really do. They light for us, not darkness."

"I love Mary," he said, touching the lamp. "When I wake up sometimes we talk to each uver."

"What do you talk about, Tommy?"

"Nice things, Mummy, nice things. Like what you say."

He smiled, closed his eyes, and drifted into slumber.

But conversations of that nature were disconcerting to Tommy's mother. She felt that some how she was being unfair to Tommy's father. He never objected to her religion or anybody else's religion excepting to insist that each person had a right to form an opinion without pressure.

So she spoke to him about it.

"I'm not trying to push my thoughts into Tommy. I only answer questions. And you know he comes out with some funny..... if you could call them funny..... remarks sometimes. You've been caught yourself."

He was understanding, spreading one palm across his eyes, in thought. " I don't suppose there's any harm either way. It's like this; I don't believe its right to tell a child anything unless what you say is correct. I had a close friendship with a psychologist a few years before I met you. He said that the first five years of a child's life patterns its adult future..... meaning the type of person, of course, not the chosen profession. I want Tommy to grow up as a proper man. You know, taking what comes and accepting it, not seeking shelter when things get tough. I don't want him asking some unknown quantity for help. To me it's foolish; you might as well ask a banana to have twins."

She pushed him into a lounge chair and sat on his lap. "I promise you that he makes his own decision. I will answer his questions as best I can and I'll never tell him that you think differently. I can't get out of my mind what you can't get into your mind. It's as simple as that."

They kissed each other. It was a type of pact.

But as she stood, he stated, his tone of voice ever – urgent, "I dearly hope that Tommy is at least twenty one before I die, sweetheart. Religious or not, he'll be a man then. I'll teach him how to take the knocks."

She pushed his forehead gently as he moved to arise after her, and as he tumbled back into the lounge she laughed. "It won't matter; you'll meet again in heaven. We all will."

He stretched an arm towards her. "Here help me up."

And as she took his hand to assist, he pulled her back onto his lap. "Heaven, he said as he kissed her again, "is right here with you and Tommy."

But talk of that nature was rare. Life had many pleasures and they found them. Tommy charmed all visitors with his winning smile and serious ways and his parents could scarcely suppress their pride. Their only concern was his disturbing fear of the dark.

Mary, his bedside angel lamp was a wonder friend. He had developed a type of devotion to it, speaking to it as if it were a human being, until one night the globe extinguished from natural usage, and his screams awakened his father to a dampened skin of perspiration.

With the main lights on, Tommy's father saw the boy sitting upright, his eyes staring. "What is it, Tommy?"

The boy held his arms outstretched to be embraced. "Mary gone black," he said. "Mary gone black angel."

"No, Tommy, angles don't have different colours. They are for everybody. Mary was tired. She had to have a sleep, too. You see, tomorrow night Mary will be just like always, she'll be awake and I'll get her a friend so they can take turns to go to sleep. Then one of them will always be awake to give you light."

Tommy accepted the remark. Eyes wide and serious, he asked. "Are there boy angels, too?" But his little heart was pounding.

"I don't know. Mummy knows. So I think we'll call Mary's friend mummie."

"Yes, Dats a good name. But I want you to come to bed wif me, Daddy,"

"If I turn the lights out and get into bed with you, will you cry because Mary is still sleeping?"

261

"No. Daddy not if you cuddle me."

So the next day Mary was blessed with a new globe; and another, slightly different angel lamp called Mummie sat on a near table. They were both switched on when Tommy retired.

Tommy's mother didn't seem unduly concerned by the incident, recounting her own discomfort in the dark which she said had not fully left her. "I remember waking up one night and crying when I was much older than Tommy. I didn't recognise any of the furnishings through the gloom and I didn't know where I was. Don't worry. It's nothing. He'll get over it."

But it worried Tommy's father. He slept with the boy for several nights with both angel lights, Mary and Mummie switched on, until he was advised that Mary and Mummie could take turns of sleeping if they wanted to.

Tommy had accepted that angels had to sleep like everybody else, and his father accepted, with silent objection, that he had no true right to criticise the firm beliefs of others of which there was no documented certainty.

His wife reminded him on one occasion, with a reminiscent smile, of their early courting days when they had been sharing childhood secrets, of how he had believed there was a man in the moon.

"If you look at the moon on some clear nights, sweetheart" he'd said, "it is easy to think that you can see the bust of a man in the bottom half. There was a story going – around when I was a kid, that if you pointed at the man in the moon he would come down and get you."

"So you pointed your finger at him."

"Yes," He'd replied with a chuckle and smile. "I would rush outside without my parents knowing, point a finger of my right hand at the moon, hold my right arm stiff with the help of my left hand to stop the trembling, then rush back and hide under the blankets."

"I'm glad he didn't come and get you," she replied.

"No. But I believed it, I truly did. And it's the only belief I ever had, I think my older brothers tidied – up the Easter Bunny, Santa Clause bits before I left the cot."

"And religion?"

"The subject never arose."

"So you couldn't really be blamed for not having a religious belief, could you?"

He'd grinned. "I don't know the answer of those thoughts. But if my parents had told me that the man in the moon was God, I would have believed it."

"Perhaps it was. I've never seen a man in the moon."

"You saw me in the moon," he'd capitalized, to close the conversation with a kiss to the cheek, "and I saw you in the moonlight."

So with Tommy's fear of the dark in abeyance, life resumed its pleasures. There was fun in the house. Tommy was moulding into the typification of the average boy being introduced to storybook characters for the first time.

"When I grow'd up proper, Daddy, I be a fixer of fings, I fink."

"What things do you want to fix, Tommy?"

"I don't know till I grow'd up, Daddy."

"But you must have some idea of what you'd like to fix."

"I fix the gate."

"What's wrong with the gate, Tommy?"

"It makes a funny noise."

"All gates make funny noises."

"I fix dem, Daddy."

"What else would you like to do when you're a man like me, Tommy?"

"I make mummies flowers grow big."

"Mummy would like that."

And as the stories were told, Tommy wanted to be a fireman, a postman, a rubbish man a bus driver, and many others.

All of them, his father mused in reflection, were outside duties; never a doctor or a dentist or a cook. All in the sunshine or the natural light of day; nothing that placed him in an area of darkness. Even the close walls of the lift whenever his mother visited his father's place of employment seemed to disturb him.

She'd make light of it in conversation. "He doesn't trust lifts. He asked me if we were going up to see God. When I said no, he hung on to one of my legs." She'd laughed. "A bit embarrassing."

His father had declined to comment. He'd been an adult before he'd entered a lift for the first time and he'd recollected that it had been a trifle unnerving. Not having a driver in command like in all other moving appliances that he'd experienced, there had been a sense of uncertainty.

What if the lift lost power and dropped to the bottom? What if it kept going and hit the roof? What if it stopped halfway and the doors opened?

He gained satisfactory answers to those qualms later on, but at the time they'd certainly been disconcerting. And he'd been an adult.

So a four year old boy hanging on to his mother's leg was understandable. He'd smiled to himself. Hanging onto any woman's leg had merit.... if she didn't push your hand away.

But that was for later, the pleasures of marriage; but to a child it was the terror of the unknown, the unseen evil that tripped you when you were running. And Tommy's father hadn't forgotten how devastating that feeling could be; the pumping of the heart, the curse of imagination, the debilitating thought of fighting it alone.

Fighting what alone? Fear. And what was the course of fear? A million different things; all tied into the process of living, of trying to control an imagination that could flare like the abandoned restrictions of a wild horse, and it's consequences.

And darkness could contain the worst of all of it, because its size was unknown until it revealed itself: it could be an elephant or a mouse.

Well, Tommy's father decided, his son was never to be left fighting the darkness alone. He telephoned an electrician.

"There's a gadget on the market," he said. "I haven't seen one but I read about it in a journal. If it's set up in the room of a child or sick person, with the other end of it in another room; you can adjust the volume to hear any sound that the child or sick person makes during the night."

"I know it," the electrician replied.

"Good, I want one hooked – up in my son's room with the listening end near the head of the bed of my wife and I. Can you do it?"

"Of course."

"Good. You purchase one and tell me a time when you'll call."

A few days later, it was in place and functioning. He explained it to his son.

"See this Tommy. It's a special thing that lets you say things to me if you wake up in the night and feel hungry or something."

"I don't feel hungry in the night, Daddy."

"Well, you might want to sing to me."

"Like when I sing... it's a wong way to tip – a – mary."

"Yes. When you sing it's a long way to Tipperary, it's a longway to go."

"I don't sing dat in the night, Daddy."

"Well, what if you wake up and Mary and Mummie have forgotten whose turn it is to go to sleep and its dark."

"I don't like dark, Daddie."

"I know, Tommy, that's why I've got this thing for you. Let's call it John. If you wake up and you want to say something to me, you call out 'Daddy' real loud, and I'll wake up and come and ask you what you want." He glanced at the bedside lamps. "Even if Mary and Mummie are still lit – up, you call me, and John will give me the message."

"How?"

"Come and I'll show you. We'll get proper Mummy to say something by your bed and we'll listen by my bed."

Proper - Mummy thought the whole arrangement was needless, but participated in the activity.

"Ho, ho, ho," she said, "this is the lady that makes the cakes."

Tommy went into a giggling fit, racing off to his own room to repeat her words. "O, O, O it's the wady what makes de cakes."

The three of them met and laughed, arms around each other.

"Now, Tommy," his father finally said. "If you wake up in the night and find that both Mary and Mummie are sleeping, you don't get frightened because it's dark. What you do, is close your eyes again and pretend you're sleeping, but you call out 'Daddy' and John will pass the message into where I am sleeping with proper mummy and I'll come to fix what you don't like."

Tommy nodded. It was another step into the future, into the light of understanding, into the bliss of contented family life. The casual comments about heaven, or God, or Angels, or fairies being cousins of angels, or Mary and Mummie being naughty for both sleeping at the same time and John having to awaken Tommy's father, were part of a routine that moulded into peace.

They were good times. Better because the General Manager of the firm where Tommy's father was employed spoke of retirement.

"I've recommended to the Board that you take – over from me," he said on one occasion. "In about twelve months. They all agreed. Unanimous decision. They all like you and you deserve the position. You might think that you're on a good salary now but imagine how you could live if it doubled."

"Good lord is it that high?"

"More than double."

"Hell. My wife believes in God I'll have to tell her," he hesitated. "I'm sorry. I forgot. You both go to the same church, don't you? She'd told you I'm not religious, I'm sure. If I were religious I'd be with her."

There was a laugh and a slap on the shoulder. "She told me you think you're an atheist."

"I am, I won't deny it. I've always been the same."

"Well, do you know what your wife thinks about you?"

"I..... I don't know. We say we love each other."

"Not that. About religion."

"I think you'd better tell me."

"Your wife thinks that you are the godliest man she'd ever known."

"Oh hell. She probably said that to not offend you. Scared you might sack me from my job."

"No, no. Nothing like that. She honestly thinks that there is more of God in you than in herself. She sees it in everything you do."

Tommy's father shook his head. "I've never known anything about religion and never wanted to."

There was another slap on the shoulder. "Religion isn't God. Religion is an expression of feelings, sentiment, a conduct of appreciation of life. But

265

no more of that talk. Let's have a whisky, I had lunch with a Japanese the other day and he gave me a bottle of their whisky that is named 'Masterpiece.' He called it 'their' whisky and I find that it's made in Canada. What do you make of that?"

They shared a grin, "let's taste it and find out. The Japanese are a long way from silly. He must work for a Canadian firm. Do you reckon?"

"I reckon it's time we tasted it."

So they sipped the whisky, spoke of the way that whisky varied in flavour from each and every country that attempted to rival Scotch whisky, that only Scotland was permitted to label their product Scotch; of how successful the commercial business in which they worked was credited on the Stock Exchange; of other miscellaneous items such as the many different shapes of the office girls legs; and what they'd do differently if they were young again.

It was an uplifting conversation that sponsored the purchase of a large iced, cream sponge cake to take home.

Tommy looked at it questionally.

"Not Mummies cake, Daddy?"

"No, Tommy. Mummy makes the little ones in the paper cups."

Tommy shook his head. "Mummy's cake, Daddy."

His mother laughed openly. "See the master of the house knows a good cook when he sees one."

"What say I give it to the kids next door? They like cake."

She agreed, but added with a smile. "Tommy knows that I make cakes in big tins too, don't you, Tommy?"

"Yum," he said with his lovely smile. "Yum, yum" rubbing at his eyes as if he preferred to see his mother's cakes.

"See," his mother remarked, he doesn't even want to look at it if it isn't mine." But that wasn't the only reason why Tommy rubbed at his eyes.

So life in the home and garden continued on its beautiful way. Mummy loved the freedom of house duties and the company of her only child, Daddy loved the thought of additional prosperity when he took – over the firm's top management, and Tommy loved life; his lovely smile, his giggles of delight when a particular incident occurred, and his parents overwhelmed all other feeling should either of them come into sight after a brief absence. He was aware that his father had to hug and wave goodbye five days of every week; and on return each afternoon a rush to the doorway at the sound of his father's footsteps on the driveway was a personal delight. He would bubble with recounting the events of the day.

It was in the latter part of Tommy's fifth year when the smile appeared to fade from his face, and his parents accepted it as a result of his introduction to kindergarten. Initially, he had enjoyed the thought of playing with other children, though much of it was due to his mother's generous description of how pleasant it would be, coupled with the 'super' fun that would occur when they were all home together again in the evening.

"We'll have so many new things to tell each other, Tommy. The things that we did when we're apart. The funny things that happened."

And it was not until the manageress of the kindergarten raised the topic before any thought was given to the boy's eyes.

"He bumps into a lot of things and rubs his right eye quite a bit," the manageress said, "have you ever had them checked?"

"What..... I..... his eyes..... no – why?" The comment had created an unexpected fright. Tommy was wonderful, the best child in the world, perfect, lovely eyes, everything.

The concern of Tommy's mother was obvious, drawing a hasty response. "Please, don't worry. I just thought I should tell you. It's my duty to report any unusual behaviour in the children, to their parents. It's just that Tommy cried today and he was rubbing at his eyes. I asked him if it was sore and he said he couldn't see properly. Well..... he said proper and them added – 'it's in the dark.' I took it that he meant his eyes were in the dark. Silly of me."

"No. No don't think that. Thank you. What ever it is I'll get it checked. I'll speak to his father."

Tommy's mother felt sick in the stomach. She called into a chemist before driving homewards and purchased an eye drop for children.

"One drop in each eye," the chemist said. "It's all you need, one drop."

"Don't worry." She tried to laugh. "I'll try it in my own eyes first."

"Good lord no, Madam. Children's eyes can be up to thirteen times stronger than adults. That bottle is clearly marked for children only, it's mild enough. But never put a child's prescription in your own eyes."

She left the shop and was pleased to be in her little V.W. car, driving towards those wonderful walls called home.

Tommy was quiet, not as cheerful as in the past.

The lady at the 'kindy' said you cried today, Tommy. Your eyes were hurting."

He nodded, not smiling.

"Are they hurting now?"

"Not when I'm wif you, Mummy."

"I bought stuff to put in your eyes. The man in the shop said it's good for little boy's eyes."

"I'll tell Daddy," he stated seriously, "Daddy fix everything."

And it wasn't easy for Tommy's mother to recount the happenings of the day to his father. Tommy rushed to the door as it opened, stretching upwards to be swept into those arms. But later in the evening she knew that she must do so.

With Tommy tucked into bed and kissed goodnight by both parents, with 'John' tested to ensure that calls for assistance safely reached the top of his parents bed, and with 'Mary' sitting by the bedside because it was her angel turn to light – up the room and give protection from any 'nasty' things that wandered around during the night; it was then that the events of the afternoon were finally aired between the two parents.

They were relaxing before the television and she reduced the sound.

Her husband looked for an explanation.

"I had a silly fright today," she said.

"I've told you before. You drive too fast in that little bomb."

"No, not that. Tommy."

"What about him?"

"I've been told to get his eyes checked."

"Hell. Who said that? He's got beautiful eyes. Like mine." He grinned at his own forced unmodesty.

"The kindergarten teacher said it. And it made me feel sick in the stomach."

"Why? Why did she say it?"

"Well. First of all she mentioned that he bumps into things that the other children pass...... but after that she said that he rubs his right eye quite a bit, and when he started to cry he said he couldn't see properly."

"He can see properly around here."

"Yes, but he knows where everything is around here."

"What is that supposed to mean?"

"They say that blind people move around their own homes without any assistance. They seem to develop a mental picture of where everything is?"

"Don't talk like that..... please." His voice had hardened. "I know he rubs his eyes now and then but that doesn't mean anything in particular. When I was a kid I had eye problems a couple of times. They turned out to be nothing. I'd wake up in the morning and my eye lids would be stuck together. I used to yell out to Mum and she'd wash around my eyes with warm water until they opened up. Sandy blight she called it."

"Did you see a doctor?"

"No. It cured itself."

"You don't think we should get them looked at?"

"Don't worry, I'll talk to the boy in the morning and find out what really troubled him. I don't like going to these special skill people. They always find something that puts, money in their pockets."

"We aren't short of money."

"Oh, hell, I didn't mean it that way, I'd give Tommy my own eyes if I could and he needed them. It's just..... I don't know what they do nowadays but years ago they used to fish eyes out with their fingers and have a look around in the socket..... without anaesthetic. Do you think I'd put Tommy through that?"

"What then?"

"I'll talk to him in the morning and find out how he really feels."

But they were both worried. The television was extinguished; they sat without speech, showered and went to bed. And during the night, on more then one occasion, they each heard the other arise and tiptoe quietly to Tommy's room to ensure that he was sleeping soundly.

And in the morning he was as bright as a button, singing jumbled words of a child's song that the kindergarten teacher had endeavoured to entice the children to sing in chorus. His parents looked at each other and breathed a sigh of relief.

"If your eye hurts you again, Tommy you will tell me won't you," his father said before giving him the usual hug and leaving for work.

"You fix, Daddy. I don't like dark."

"Yes, Tommy. If it hurts you tell me and I'll fix."

"You promise?"

"Yes, Tommy, I promise."

"A big promise, Daddy?"

"Yes, Tommy. A big, big, big promise"

Tommy smiled, but it was not his old smile; the beautiful smile that his father had thought he had seen through the glass pane of that hospital where the boy had been born..... the smile had been claimed by his father, less than an hour after that exciting birth.

But Tommy's mother saw something withdrawn on the boy's smile, something that she didn't like, something that no child should ever have to bear. And without sound reason, tears poured from her eyes, and she drew her sleeve across her face to soak the moisture in an effort to conceal the anguish of her imagination before Tommy saw them.

"You got sore eye and dark, too, Mummy?"

"No, Tommy." She hugged him. "Mummy only a silly girl. Girl's cry when they're happy, too."

"Daddy fix you, too, Mummy. Like he promise me."

"Yes, Tommy. Daddy fix all our pain and we won't cry ever again."

"And dark, Mummy?"

"Yes, and dark. Like he does when 'Mary' and 'Mummie' go to sleep at the same time." But as she spoke she was praying, silently, praying in her mind.

"Oh, God, dear God, let it be nothing that will tear us all apart. I beg of you. Please tell me that my little boy's eyes are sound."

But God did not answer her plea.

Nor did she take Tommy to the kindergarten that day, she was frightened. And she hoped she would never have to tell her husband the reason for her fears. As a child, not many years older than Tommy, something had been said over the dinner table in her parent's home in England, to which she had given no further thought..... until now.

Had she deliberately blocked it out or had it held no significance, she didn't know. But she did know that memories could be as cruel as they could be kind.

Perhaps they should all have a holiday. They'd never bothered with annual holidays, they'd been happy to have all of that extra time together. She'd speak to Tommy's father about it.

But a few days passed and the approaching Christmas period began to fill the air.

The manageress of the kindergarten made an announcement. "I'm arranging for a photographer to call and take us all together. These memories are so lovely to look back on in later years."

Tommy's parents applauded the intention; it was something for future memories. As adults, the children of today could fan through those photographs and wonder about the progress of the other children, where they were, what they had achieved, did they have happy marriages, anything, everything.

So the photographer called as arranged, though could not 'take' the children outdoors owing to unpleasant weather, but did so indoors with a flash lamp.

There was laughter and giggles and mild ejaculations as the flash filled the air.

"There's more," the photographer said. "I need to take a few and pick the best one where you all look beautiful."

Which he did, and there was more laughter.

Tommy thought it was exciting. "A great big light, Mummy," he said, in reference to the flash.

And a few days later, on collection of each child at the close of kindergarten the parent was handed a copy of the little group as a complimentary gesture.

Tommy wanted the photograph to sit on the cabinet beside his bed where 'Mary' was in charge; so a photo stand was purchased to give it prominence.

"When you're grown – up like Daddy," his mother said, "all your little playmates will be grown – up, too, and you can talk about the games you played together."

"And singing," Tommy added.

"Yes. And singing."

But the excitement of that photograph must have disturbed Tommy, because his crying during the night awakened his father who spent the remainder of those hours of rest curled into the bed with the boy cuddled into his arms.

In the morning, Tommy was bright but not smiling. "'Mary' shines on my friends now," he said to his mother.

But his mother's earlier worries, the thumping of the heart, the sickness in the stomach, the fear, were destined to return again.

The telephone rang mid – morning. "Yes," she said.

"Do you remember a blond..... what I've got left of it..... skinny bloke about thirty five who collected his child at the same time as you the other day..... at the kindergarten?"

"Yes, yes, of course. "We both said good afternoon. she laughed. "At the same time, I think. Can I help you?"

"Well I was hoping that I could help you. I was thinking of your little boy."

Her heart lurched. "Tommy?"

"Yes. I believe that's his name. I described him to the people at the kindergarten and they gave me your name and address..... and, of course, Tommy's."

"You've lost me, I'm afraid. How can you help Tommy or me? Do we need help that we don't know about?"

"Well, that's why I'm ringing. I'm an ophthalmologist."

"Gosh. What are they?"

"Eye specialists."

She was seated but her hand flattened on the table to steady herself. Words locked in her throat."

"Are you still there?"

"Yes." she managed.

"I wondered if Tommy was receiving treatment. I wouldn't interfere."

"I don't understand," she said, not recognising her own voice.

It was his turn to delay speech. "I've come at this the wrong way," he stated in an apologetic tone. "I'm sorry."

"Come at what the wrong way? Tell me. Please tell me. What is it?"

"Something I noticed in that photograph of the children taken in their schoolroom. Do you have one?"

"Yes, of course. Please, please, what of it?"

"I may be wrong. I'm a fool. I thought I was doing a favour and I know I'm upsetting you."

"You aren't upsetting me. I'm upsetting myself. But I must know what it is."

There was another pause. "Do you have that photograph with you?"

"I'll get it."

She returned. "What about it?"

"It was taken by a flash lamp."

"I don't know for sure. I wasn't there. But Tommy mentioned a big light and all the children laughing."

"Look at the photograph."

"Yes."

"Look at the childrens' eyes."

"Yes."

"Do you notice any difference in Tommy's?"

She stared intently at the photograph, lowering it to the table to forego the shake in her hand. "They.... they're a bit different to the other children, I think."

There was another pause. "Perhaps I should duck out to see you. I could close the office. No trouble."

"No. More. Please. Tell me."

"Very well. But you must understand that I could be quite wrong."

"Please, just tell me. You're stalling around."

"When flashlight's are used in photography they often reflect in a manner that we call a 'cat's eye reflex,' that is if the cameras are without red – eye reduction."

"What does that mean?"

"A normal retina reflects a red colour in a flash light photograph that is if the camera doesn't have red – eye reduction."

"Yes."

"Are Tommy's red?"

"No, not really. They're whitish. He has lovely eyes."

"Are the other children's retinas red?"

"Yes. Yes I suppose they are."

"Red is the normal situation."

"You said that before." Her elbow rested on the table, the butt of her free hand shoving up at her forehead.

Tommy entered the room, running to her. "Don't cry, Mummy, don't cry."

"A white reflection instead of red is a sign of tumour. It could be just the way he was holding his head, or a window or something casting a strange light on his face. But it is in both eyes."

"Don't cry, Mummy, please don't cry."

"Thank you for calling," She heard herself say, before reaching to pull Tommy onto her lap, hugging him, kissing him, and hating the news that she would have to impart to her husband.

"Let us play sleepy, byes, Tommy." she said. "We'll curl up on the bed and cuddle off to sleep."

The urge to telephone her husband and ask him to return home early was strong, but she resisted it. She had much to say and it would be better said after Tommy had said goodnight to 'Mary' before he was tucked into his bed that evening.

So once again, relaxing after the evening meal before the television, she stretched to deaden its sound.

"I have something to tell you," she said, "and when I do you will hate me."

"I will never hate you, I love you. And I guess it's because your face has lost it colour."

"I've never told you much about my parents, have I?"

"No. But I don't suppose I've told you much about my own. They've both passed away."

"Mine are in England, I've told you that."

"Yes. They came out with that scheme to populate the country. Populate or perish they called it. Ten pounds is all that they had to pay for the passage so long as they stayed for at least two years."

"Yes. They stayed for twenty years. I was born here. When I was self reliant and other relatives in England were asking my parents when they planned to return, they finally left."

"So what about them?"

"It's something I'd forgotten but it came back to me today. I truly wished I could die. I wanted to die."

"Oh, come on." He placed an arm around her and pulled her near. "Nothing is that bad."

"Yes, it is. I didn't think anything could be that bad, but I was wrong."

"You'd better tell me or I'll be the one to die."

"We were at the dinner table once when I was about six or seven, and my father read part of a letter that he'd received from his family in England. He was reading it to my mother and I really didn't pay much attention, but I heard him say, 'Charlie's dead. They think it was suicide.'"

"Who was Charlie?"

"My Uncle."

"Why would he suicide? If he did suicide."

"My mother asked my father the same question."

"And."

273

"My father said, 'you knew he was blind. They removed his eyes when he was about five. He had tumours behind them."

"Good God, at that age. The poor bugger."

"The cancer had spread. They controlled it, but my uncle couldn't tolerate the darkness. When he was about seventeen they found him at the bottom of a cliff, and he knew the path that lead to it like he knew the back of his hand."

"So it probably was suicide."

"Yes." Her taunt, controlled speech that he had admired from their first meeting in the public gardens many years before left her. She turned her face into his shoulder and burst into tears.

"Come on, come on." He found that he was patting her back as if she were a child.

She breathed heavily several times then straightened. "My Uncle's complaint is called Retinoblastoma and it is genetic. I had a telephone call from a father of one of the children who goes to Tommy's kindergarten. I rang him back and asked how it occurs."

"So why does that upset you."

"I think I've passed it on to Tommy."

She felt his body stiffen. He was frozen, the fingers of the hand behind her tightening into her flesh until it hurt, but she made no comment.

"It can't be," he finally said. "It's wrong. Tommy's just a little boy. The man must be a fool. I'll ring him tomorrow. He shouldn't say things like that. He's after money, that's what he's after."

"No. I've made an appointment for tomorrow morning. The three of us."

Without speech, he stooped to remove his shoes and tiptoe to Tommy's room to kiss the boy's cheek. On return, he asked. "How did this fellow know? He could be wrong. He hasn't seen Tommy. Has he? What is he? A communist. Someone who doesn't like people to have a happy life?" His voice was jerking.

"Please. He's a good man. I spoke to him at the kindergarten. He doesn't want money. He has a little girl of his own. He knows how we would feel. He's an ophthalmologist."

"What the hell are they? Invaders from Mars?"

"Please. He's trying to help. He saw the difference in Tommy's retinas in that photograph they took at the kindy. He knows that he might be wrong. He was really hoping that we were having treatment now. That's why he rang, but he said that he knew from when he started to speak to me we weren't."

He hugged her. "I'm sorry. It was stupid of me. I should be grateful. How do they treat these things? If the worst is the worst, Tommy can have my eyes. They must be able to transplant eyes. They can transplant every other God damned thing nowadays, Tommy can have both my eyes if needs be, I've seen enough. Too much I'd say."

"Let us wait," she said. "I don't think they can transplant eyes. But we could be thinking the wrong way, let us go to bed. You lift Tommy into our bed..... between us. He loves that."

So the next day they kept their appointment with the ophthalmologist. They travelled by train and Tommy enjoyed standing on the seat with both palms and his nose flattened on the window pane. On one occasion, the boy turned, placed a hand over his right eye and said, with a wisp of a smile, "see better, Daddy. You fix Daddy?"

"Yes, Tommy," he answered slowly reaching to hold his wife's hand, "Daddy fix."

At the consultation rooms, drops were put into Tommy's eyes to dilate the pupils, but only after Tommy had heard his father say. "Nice man help Daddy fix."

With his mother and father each holding a hand Tommy tolerated what was asked of him though in a very reluctant and frightened manner.

After what seemed an eternity, the ophthalmologist patted Tommy, said he'd been a good boy, and turned towards the parents.

"How long," he said, "how long have you let this go on?"

They both stared. What? Were they being accused of neglect?

"You'd better spell it out," Tommy's father finally said.

"One must go, quickly. I can tell you that. The other one, I don't know yet. Tomorrow, no later. I'll take them out under general anaesthetic, see what's there, and put them back again. I'll know then if the second one must go. I'll also arrange a lumbar puncture to see if it's spread. Heavens above, didn't you notice. This disease is passed through the genes. There must have been family trouble before."

"Yes, Tommy's mother answered both her voice and her body trembling with fear and apprehension self – blame. "It's my fault. I was a little girl myself when I heard about it and it didn't come back to me until we spoke over the telephone yesterday. An uncle of mine in England had it, I think. He lost both eyes."

"What happened?"

"He committed suicide at seventeen. He couldn't tolerate the darkness, and there were complications, I believe. My husband and I had no knowledge of these sorts of things in our own lives. What can we do now?"

"Bring our little friend in tomorrow at ten o'clock. We'll see." He patted Tommy's head. "You come and see me again tomorrow."

"Daddy bring me," Tommy stated, lurching to catch he's father's hand as the dilated pupils from the specialists eye drops impaired his vision even further. "Hold me, Daddy," he added.

His father stooped to lift the boy to let him sit saddlewise above the hip, and silently they left the building and caught a taxi to their home.

They each were frightened, scared to speak and not knowing what to say if they did.

"You blamed yourself and that wasn't fair;" he stated, after he had opened the door and they were all safely inside. "I guess it is from your side of things and maybe you would have known if you'd gone to England with your parents. But you didn't go back. You stayed here and we met and you gave me a beautiful boy I love you both. I'm older than you and I certainly didn't know about the problem. One child in seventeen thousand, he said. That number mightn't mean much if you're talking about apples on a tree, but kids throughout the world. Hell. Every mother should get a story about it as soon as a child is born."

She heard his comments in silence, still too frightened to speak: Tommy had moved off to his room and they heard him talking to 'Mary' about the man who put water in his dark eye. Daddy fix, he had added.

His father spoke again. "We have to wait until tomorrow before we really know the situation."

"He said 'one must go,'" she asked. "He didn't mean..... not..... did he?"

"Yes." There was a savagery in his tone. "He did mean that." He, too, was frightened to mention the action implied. "And Tommy is expecting me to fix it. Dear God, I hope that doctor was wrong."

"You said God. That's not like you. I think that God stopped us from having a second child. They say there's nothing wrong with us."

"I didn't mean it that way," he answered. "It's an expression, that's all." There was a ring of anger in his tone. "God, bloody God. You know I don't believe in that tripe. Why did your God have to wait until Tommy was born before he waved his famous wand? He only has to wave it once in every seventeen thousand births. Even I could do that."

"Please." She took his arm. "Don't let us quarrel. I'll make some tea."

"Yes. Do that. Make it strong. I wasn't quarrelling." He was bumping the palm of one hand against his forehead. "You know, I've never had a religion and it all seems so damned ridiculous. More so when things like this occur. Do you know what I have to do if the doctor repeats what he said today, after he does his test tomorrow?"

She turned. He knew that she was trembling and he hated it. He loved her, had loved her from that first moment on the park seat when she'd excused herself before leaving. He didn't want to hurt her in any way. Yes, she was religious and he wasn't. And yes he wasn't religious because it hadn't been part of his formative years; those years when you believed everything that your parents said.

"What do you have to do?" she asked.

"Fix Tommy. That's what I have to do."

She ran the few steps between them, a flood of tears in her eyes. Her face fell against his chest and her arms around him.

"I will pray for you. I will pray and pray and pray."

He held her tight. "Don't pray. What ever has to be done, I will do. It's too late for one of these miracles that they write about in books. Tommy will hate me if it's what we think. It will destroy our love and I won't blame him. He will ask me why I let the doctor place him in the darkness he has always feared."

"No," she looked up. "The genes are mine. I must tell him."

He shook his head, "Daddy fix. Remember, I said I would fix. We should all have two lives. We learn so much in our first life when it is too late to use the knowledge."

He kissed the top of her hair. "How suddenly three happy lives can be destroyed," she heard him say, but he was speaking his thoughts, to himself, so she did not comment.

The following morning they silently dressed to make their return trip to the ophthalmologist.

"We have to go back to see the man in the white coat, Tommy," his father said as his mother carefully dressed him. "The nice man we saw yesterday."

Tommy nodded. "Can I take 'Mary'," he asked quietly.

His father felt his body jerk. It was an unexpected request, almost unsuited to the occasion. "But Mary won't light up when she's outside; Mary is your night time friend."

"Please, Daddy." There were tears in the boy's eyes. "Mary won't want the light out there."

Tommy's father blinked the tears that rushed to his own eyes. "Of cause you can take Mary, she might like a ride in the taxi car. I'll put her in a bag for you."

"I want to hold her, Daddy, all tight. Like you hold me."

"Then I'll have to pull Mary's funny old tail out of the wall and wrap it tight around her."

"I love you, Daddy."

"And I love you, Tommy."

He rushed to his bedroom and closed the door, but his wife followed. She'd never seen her husband cry before, and she sat beside him on the edge of the bed, not speaking, even when he took and squeezed her hand. "How can I possibly authorise a doctor to remove Tommy's eye," he choked out. "Or maybe both of them. I wish so much that they could transplant eyes, but they can't. I'd rather die than say those words. Jump off the harbour bridge. Anything. And why did Tommy ask to take that lamp we named Mary? He's never wanted to take it outside before."

She didn't reply, she had no answer.

So they arrived at the doctors to be welcomed by a friendly nurse who understood Tommy's refusal to release his grasp of Mary. There was a fear in his reaction to the movement around him and only the friendliness of the nurse allayed those fears.

The anaesthetic was administered without the boy's knowledge and when he was still in the company of his parents. And they were called to be present as he awakened.

"It is as I expected," the ophthalmologist said as they waited for Tommy to regain consciousness. "We can't do anything with the right eye. There's a growth over three quarters' of it and another part – formed on the left. I've taken a lumber puncture to discover if the cancer has spread and that'll take a few days. By then I'll know the future of the left eye, also. I know you're worried but I want you to appreciate that the teachers in schools for the blind are absolutely marvellous, dedicated people. Lots of them have family or know somebody close with similar problems. When I get the results back I'll let you know without delay. By Monday I'd say."

It was a warm day but Tommy's parents were cold, both shivering. They caught a taxi to their home and were pleased to walk into it. They made a pot of tea, and Tommy chose to go back to bed with Mary clutched tightly to his chest. Both parents kissed him as if it were night time, and his father shifted 'Mummie' from her small table near one wall and plugged the angel bed light in Mary's usual location. It was turned on.

"He knows there's something wrong," his father said as they sat sipping tea in the kitchen. "He's too quiet. He's hugging that lamp as if it were a teddy bear or something."

"I'll ask God," she said. "Down at the church."

"Oh, please. None of that. I'm not in the mood for it."

She stood. "I'll go now. You take care of Tommy."

He didn't object. If comfort was anywhere, let it be felt.

After she had left, he checked to find Tommy sound asleep, then sat quietly thinking. He was shattered of spirit, mentally powerless. Only one thing was certain in his mind, and that was his life long declaration that he would never go back on his word. He could hear Tommy's voice tumbling through his mind. "You promise, Daddy, you promise."

The pain in his imagination hurt him. Like a knife, it cut at him, and he made a decision.

He telephoned his place of employment and asked if the chairman was engaged or still in his office. The switchboard operator put his call through, the chairman was aware of a family desire to be home, and was disinclined to be jovial. Pleasantries were passed over.

"About a year ago at a luncheon," he said to the chairman, "I met am ex – army Colonel friend of yours, Richard something or other, I had quite a long conversation with him."

"Yes, Richard Larney. Passed every examination there was to pass in the army. Had to wait for someone to die to go up a peg. What about him?"

"Do you know his address? I need to ask him something."

"No. But I have his telephone number. Is that good enough."

"Yes. Better."

"Hang on and I'll dig it out." There were a few moments of silence before a number was relayed over the wire."

"Thanks."

"I'm keeping my seat warm for you."

"With that big bum of yours." It was an effort at humour,

They hung up their telephones and a call was made to the ex – army Colonel and friendship renewed.

When his wife returned from visiting the church, she found him sitting at Tommy's bedside reading. There was more colour in her cheeks than when she'd left and with a desire to be less critical than with the remarks he'd made over the past couple of days, he said. "It seems as if it were worth your while. You've been so darned pale it troubled me."

"Yes. I saw Tommy in heaven "

He shook his head. "Please, sweetheart, don't turn into one of these crackpots. Tommy's alive. He's sound asleep. He's here with us. Don't go nutty on me."

"I'm not going nutty on you. I simply know that Tommy is going to be okay."

"Look. Spooks can't cure cancer. You know that. I don't want you to say those things. You might think that they help but they don't. I'm sick in the stomach and I'm trying to keep my mind off everything and I can't. I've read the same page twenty times. On a couple of occasions, I tried to walk around the room with my eyes shut. It was horrible. Losing one eye is frightening enough but to lose them both..... I don't know, I just don't know. And there's this lumber puncture."

"We haven't got the results yet. It mightn't be as bad as we think. People always imagine the worst. You can't help doing that. It's the way we are."

"Will you make some tea." It was a diversion from the nature of conversation.

"Of course."

He watched her leave the room. Her steps were more sprightly than they had been for two days. One thing about religion, he had to admit, it was good for those who could believe it. He almost smiled with his own recollections; his childhood thoughts that there was a man in the moon.

He kissed Tommy softly and moved to the kitchen to share a pot of tea with his wife. "Tomorrow," he said "I have to make a quick run up to the Blue Mountains."

"Oh." she was surprised. "Can we come?"

"I'd love it, but I think you should stay with Tommy. He's been pretty low these past two days. Do you mind?"

"What ever you think. Is it business?"

He hesitated, "In a way. I want to talk to a fellow I met at a luncheon."

"You'll drive."

"I'd better. I don't know where the house is situated. I suppose I could catch a train then a taxi."

"Do that, it's safer."

But in the morning Tommy didn't want him to leave. "Don't go, Daddy, my eye aches. The man in de white coat hurt it."

"He didn't mean to hurt you, Tommy. He was trying to make it better."

"You fix it, Daddy?"

"I'll try, Tommy, I'll try hard."

"You promise?"

"I promise like I said before."

So Tommy's father travelled to the Blue Mountains, had lunch with the ex – army Colonel and his wife, and returned home late in the afternoon. He was both sad and pleased with the happenings of the day..... and certainly pleased to kiss his wife and sweep Tommy into his arms when the door to his home opened.

The next two days, Thursday and Friday he stayed home, waiting for a telephone call from the ophthalmologist, embracing his wife every time she was near, and playing with Tommy. He hated the moments when Tommy's hand would lift to rest over his right eye for a few moments before he would take it away and continue what he was doing.

No longer was the boy jovial, no longer did he smile, never did he say that he wanted to be a gardener or a policeman or a milkman..... when he 'growed – up.'

And it hurt; it hurt his mother, it hurt his father; and it hurt the air in the room.

On the Monday, the telephone finally rang. Could they call in to see the specialist. Anytime would do. Only one of them if they preferred, and preferably the father.

Tommy didn't want to make another visit to the nice man in the white coat, so his father went alone; caught in a sickening slow traffic jam.

The specialist asked if he would like a cup of tea or coffee and he thought he'd said 'no thanks' but a cup of coffee was set before him on a small table in the waiting room. He rarely drank coffee but a sip revealed it to be very sweet so he drank it. Somehow, he felt that they were waiting for him to finish it before he was invited to move into the doctor's private room.

There was a hand shake and a gesture at a chair.

"I'm glad you came alone," the ophthalmologist said. "Sometimes women become quite distraught when I tell them what is necessary to say."

He nodded. "It was Tommy. He didn't want to come. My wife is strong, stronger than me I think, sometimes. I have to swallow my feelings and pretend."

"I must tell you the worst and I have to be truthful."

"Please do, I must know."

"The right eye must be removed and it is my opinion that the same should happen to the left. You could get a second opinion there if you wished and I could recommend an excellent man. But I know what he would say. And the lumber puncture was not good."

The mouth of Tommy's father was dry, but he managed. "Is this because we..... I left it too late?"

"Perhaps, perhaps not. Do you have older children."

"No Tommy is the first..... and last."

"It is often that way. What first time parents know how a baby should behave unless they're had some experience, is not easy to assess."

"He was always so bright."

"When it's caught early, we can almost always cure it. But it must be early. Retinoblastoma, I mean."

"So we're been neglectful parents."

"No, no, never think that. You mustn't blame yourselves."

"Thank you." Tommy's father stood, then clutched at the desk to steady himself. "I'll talk to my wife."

Suddenly he was out in the street, walking, and he could not recall how he entered the lift to do so. Nor did he know how he could repeat the news.

Where he walked, down which street he walked, he also did not know; but late that afternoon he found that Tommy had run to greet him and the little boy was in his arms.

"Daddy home," he said, "Daddy home."

And that evening, with 'Mary' casting her subdued lighting over the boy's sleeping figure the two parents sat again before a silenced television.

"No change, sweetheart," Tommy's father recorded. "The right eye has gone too far it seems. A tumour is covering the majority of the retina and the left eye isn't far behind."

"Is there nothing we can do?"

"So he says. Chemotherapy might help the left eye and it might not. But there are other concerns."

"Oh, lord, not into the body."

"He mentioned the lymph glands. Frankly I don't recall what he said about that. I was so shocked with what I'd heard before. Dear little Tommy. How could I possibly explain it to the boy? He thinks I can fix everything. He'll hate me. Do you realize that. He'll hate me. Ever since he's been able to talk he's been afraid of the dark and now I'm due to place him in it forever. I can't do it, sweetheart, I can't do it. He's too young to understand. I'll never be able to explain."

He buried his face in his hands, his shoulders shaking as he sobbed. "It's wrong, it's wrong. These past few years have been wonderful. You, Tommy, me all together. The world's a bastard, that's what it is, a bastard."

She placed a hand gently on his shoulder, almost frightened to touch him. "It's all my fault, not yours. That day, in the park, I said I'd give you a son. And what have I done. I've tortured all of us. I'll never go near that church again. I promise you."

"No, please," he turned to hug her. "Never say that. Your comfort will be there. Me I don't know. I think I envy you. Where would I turn if I didn't have you? I have nowhere to turn. You have your faith, and my faith is in you. You gave me Tommy. Never blame yourself. Your genes maybe. But who knows. What do I know about my family history. Nothing, that's what, nothing. We were poor and my father conducted himself like a gentleman. That's all I know. We could have had this rotten thing in us, too."

"It's not you," she answered slowly. "It's my fault. I know it."

"Fault, fault. Is being born a fault?"

"The minister said that we have to be born before we can go to heaven."

"Heaven, heaven was here, in this home. Where is that beautiful smile of Tommy's? Have you seen it in the last six months?"

"Yes. Every evening when he hears your footsteps at the door."

"Yes. True. But it didn't last. I've been stupid, sweetheart. Since early days he's been afraid of the dark. I never thought that his eyes might have something to do with it. I don't know now, really. We all know that some people are born blind. But most of us think that eyes simply got weaker with age. I know an optometrist. He's a member of the sports club. You know what he said to me one day..... he said, 'we get them all at forty.' I took that to be the norm. He meant the need for glasses. But hell, how dumb can a man be."

She moved her arm across his shoulder as a message. "What do we do? Tommy has to be told. We can't just put him into hospital and let him wake up with no sight."

"It's my problem. I'm his father. I've let him think I can fix all of his little troubles. I rang the eye hospital, I thought we might be able to have something done overseas. England, America, Russia. But they said we're got the latest knowledge here."

"What can I do?"

"Nothing. You go to bed, I'll sit here for awhile."

"Then I'll sit with you. In bed, I want your arms around me."

He kissed her and pulled the cheek of her face to his chest.

Later, he arose, stretched a hand to assist her to her feet, and hugged her. She was silent, but wishing that he had religion to lean on, to provide an escape from the cold reality of what he soon must face.

Neither of them slept that night, each of them feigning sleep but constantly arising to check Tommy in his slumber, and not speaking when the other returned.

He was cold – eyed in the morning, lifting Tommy to his lap at the breakfast table and letting the boy share his cereal. That had been an early routine that they'd weaned out at about two years with the introduction of a high chair.

She made no comment.

He didn't dress for work nor did he charge from his dressing gown.

She let that pass, too. If he wanted to say anything to her, she knew he would say it.

There was thick pile on the carpet in the lounge room and he sat there playing with Tommy. At ten o'clock she brought them both a warm drink.

"Thanks," he said as he raised both hands to take the drinking vessels. Then, "I want you to do something for me."

"Of cause. Anything at all."

"I have to advise the chairman on a certain matter. Will you take it in, I've written it out? Only an envelope."

"About your trip to the Blue Mountains?"

"Yes. In a way. Will you do it this morning?"

"You'll take care of Tommy. And will I indicate how much time you might be away from work?"

"No. It's in the letter. Don't leave it at reception. Give it to him personally."

283

"I'll do it now. The sooner I leave, the sooner I return." She moved off in order to change her clothing.

He handed her a stiff, brown envelope. "Better if he reads it while you're there. Could be an answer."

He placed his arms around her to hold her warmly before kissing her lips. "See what Daddy did, Tommy. Mummy has to go into town for me and I want you to give her a nice big kiss and a cuddle like Daddy did."

Tommy performed. "That's a good mummy," he said.

She left, wistfully looking back and waving before she closed the door, hating to leave them for even a minute; the pain of an unjust future tearing at her heart.

"I love you," her husband called. "We love you very much."

She hesitated, only part hearing his words as she made off on the short walk to the railway station; the train was the quickest way, she thought. No traffic to tolerate with her clouded mind, no parking spot to find for the car.

For a short while after she'd left, Tommy and his father sat on the carpet, rolling a soft ball back and forth to each other, then Tommy said. "Cuddle me, Daddy, my eye hurts."

Tommy crawled across to the opened arms.

"Has Mummy ever told you about heaven, Tommy?"

"Yes, Daddy. Nuffing dark in heaven, Mummy said. Proper angels not like 'Mary and Mummie' but proper – proper what talk. No hurt in the eye or anything."

"Would you like to go to heaven, Tommy?"

The boy shook his head. "No Daddy. Only if you there."

"Promise."

"Yes, I promise."

"After you fix my eye from the pain and the dark."

"No, Tommy, we go there to fix it."

"Do they fix eyes in heaven?"

"In heaven they fix everything. Tommy."

"Will Mummy come."

"Mummy will come after."

Tommy smiled. "Mummy's a good mummy."

His father drew the sleeve of his dressing gown across his eyes. "Mummy is a wonderful mummy, Tommy."

And in the mean while, Tommy's mother sat in a train, twisting a handkerchief around and around in her fingers. Life, love, joy, pain. God, was there really a God. Had she been deluding herself on all of those occasions when she'd thought that God had placed this thoughts into her mind, guided her, patterned a way of life for her.

The day in the park when the man to be her husband had sat on the bench beside her, not speaking, quiet, keeping full distance from her..... and yet she'd returned the next day in the hope of seeing him and missing out because she'd made a visit to the church to seek a message. And she had received a message. Or had she? Had she been putting thoughts into her own mind. Telling herself what she wanted to feel and convincing herself that God had guided her.

But he too had gone back that second day, hoping to see her. Why? Had God guided him, and he didn't know?

He didn't believe in God, he'd said later, nor Santa Clause nor Easter Bunny. He'd believed that he could see a man in the moon during his early childhood and truly thought that if he pointed at that man he would come down and get him. Get him? What did that mean? Take him back into the moon?

And what had he done, that husband of hers. He'd pointed a finger, holding his arm stiff with his free hand, then racing back to his bed, shaking with fright. And thankful that the man had not seen him, looking the other way, perhaps.

Could that have been the beginning of a type of religion of its own?

The train was slowing and there were flashes of lights and signs and Martin Place, the wall sign indicated. She could have missed it.

A short walk to the work place of her husband. He was popular there. Popular most everywhere, she thought.

What would they be doing now? She glanced at her wrist watch, a beautiful watch. Her husband had given it to her on their first wedding anniversary; gold with inset diamonds skirting around the dial case.

What would they be doing? Well, let her think. They'd be standing on the plastic sheet with the many footprints on it all painted in different directions. The idea was to see how many footprints one could step onto without falling over. And Tommy loved it because his father fell over trying to be too clever and Tommy always won.

They were such good pals, those two.

She reached the reception desk and asked if she could see the chairman. They all knew her; the receptionist giving a smile of welcome at first sight.

"You know the office, I think," the receptionist said after she'd spoken "level eight."

She caught the lift and the chairman was in the foyer to greet her as she alighted. He kissed her cheek. "You weren't at church on Sunday. Had me worried. Not a miss for years."

"Little things at home. Tommy really."

They walked into a spacious office. There was a gesture towards a copious lounge. "You'll have tea.. coffee?"

"Tea, please."

"What brought you in?"

"Gosh. I nearly forgot." She extracted the envelope from her purse. "I'm the messenger girl. I think it's about his run up to the Blue Mountains."

He took the envelope and tossed it onto his desk, before opening the doors to a cabinet that revealed a miniature kitchen. "I can get it sent up but I like to make my own." Meaning the drinks.

He glanced back at the envelope as if to bring it into significance. "They had a nice day up there. The Colonel gave me a call. Said it was about time I made the trip." He turned to lift a delicate willow teapot. 'strong or weak?'

It was pleasant, breezy conversation that she would have enjoyed under other circumstances, but it was obvious that he knew little or nothing about Tommy's complaint.

"Strong today," she answered softly.

He laughed. "Strong today. No worries surely." He waved one hand about in a sweeping gesture. "In six month's time, I'll be sailing off to Europe with my wife and your husband will be sitting here treating you to anything you'd like..... I'll let you add your own milk and sugar."

"You don't know about Tommy do you?" she said.

"Of course I know Tommy. You bring him to church with you each Sunday."

"I mean why Charles is away from work."

He lowered the teapot and looked at her. "It's something serious, isn't it?"

Tears gushed into her eyes, the agony of the past few days finally overwhelming her. "Tommy has Retinoblastoma, tumours behind his eyes. One eye has to come out and the other soon, I think." She knew that her whole body was shaking; trying to be strong in the company of her husband when his anguish was exposed, had been bad enough, but to relate it herself, in words, had been too much.

She cried openly, and copiously, the chairman's arms around her for human support, for warmth, for fatherly understanding.

"God, he never said a word. How is he taking it?" He reached for a linen napkin. "How is Charles taking it?"

"Dreadfully. He cannot see how he can possible give an authority for Tommy's eyes to be removed, Tommy worships him, trusts him in every way."

"Is there nothing you can do?"

"They say it is too late. And the cancer could be elsewhere."

"On Sunday I'll ask the minister to have prayers for them, both of them."

"Charles won't be there. He has never had religion in him and yet it bubbles out of him."

"I know. I'll ring him now. He can have all the time off that he wants. Weeks, months, it doesn't matter. I'll delay my retirement."

He left her and moved to his desk on which there were three phones. He flipped a telephone index and rang a number, lifting a hand in acknowledgement as she mentioned her own home number. But he was speaking to the Colonel. And she heard.

"You issued them to the soldiers in New Guinea during the war. When the Japs were there. When they were doing a patrol into Japanese territory. Better to end it quick rather than be brutalised. Yes, yes, Colonel. I've got that, too. Thank you."

He closed the phone and made another quick call. "There's nobody answering at your home." he said. "Would Charles have gone out?"

"I don't think so. He was playing with Tommy. They were both in their pyjamas."

The Chairman looked at his telephone index again. He was moving quickly, as if in desperate urgency, it seemed.

"Minister, please, it's Wentworth here. Little Tommy, you know him. He speaks to you of a Sunday. You know his mother's address. Get down there quickly. Break in. Get the police. Anybody, just get in. I'll meet you there."

She was staring at him, "what is it?"

He was reaching for a different phone. "My car and chauffeur out the front immediately, two minutes, no longer."

She repeated herself. "What is it?'

"Do you have a large dog?"

"Dogs aren't allowed in our street."

He tore open the envelope that she'd delivered. "Good God," he said, "Good God."

"What is it, please, what is it?"

"Charles met the colonel at a dinner party some time back. Colonel happened to mention that he had been issued with a bottle of pills to dispense to the troops before they undertook dangerous reconnaissance into Japanese territory. You've seen films depicting how the Japanese treated their prisoners. The colonel told Charles that he still had them in a medicine chest"

"What do they do?"

"They kill you in seconds when swallowed."

She couldn't speak, her face a ghostly white.

287

"And Charles.... he what?"

"He said he had a very, large old dog in rheumatic pain and he wanted to put it down. He asked for two tablets."

Suddenly, as if carried in a whirlwind, as if she were living her life over again, as it tumbled through her mind, she found herself walking along the path that led to her home of those past, wonderful five years.

There were a few people standing quietly at each side but she did not see them. There were others inside but she saw only the church minister from where she had attended with Tommy.

He came towards her. "They looked so beautiful," he said in his palative, sermon tone of voice. "I have blessed them."

Somehow she knew that she should go to Tommy's room. Her stomach was knotted but she was emptied of tears, her face white and her body cold.

The minister was beside her. "That beautiful smile," he murmured from his ability to see beauty in death. "They have gone to heaven together."

The fingers of her hands were grinding emptiness as she looked at them, side by side on Tommy's bed, facing each other, caught between them the two angel – lamps that had been named 'Mary and Mummie.'

There was indeed a beautiful smile on Tommy's face, the happy, affectionate smile of youth that had somehow frozen as he looked into his father's eyes; and his father wore his old expression of satisfaction, of take it as it comes, of contentment.

She stopped to gently kiss their cheeks, to touch their skin with her fingertips.

And she was cold, freezing cold, almost too cold to move, her hand trembling.

Why wasn't she crying? The question entered her mind and stayed there, unanswered. She wanted to cry, expected to cry, but she wasn't. Perhaps she was too hurt to cry: the mental hurt, so different from the physical pain of injury. The hurt that no aspirin could cure.

How long did she stand there, she didn't know. Gently, once again, she ran her soft fingers over their faces; following their cheeks down to, and beneath their chins, gracing their neck lines.

Did the lips of Charles move? Did she hear him say "I love you." He's said it often for no special reason.

She'd enter a room sometimes when he was reading, and he'd look up to say "I love you, sweetheart," then he'd return to his reading.

"Thank you," she'd reply with a smile.

But he wouldn't hear, he was reading again.

Stoic of face, she left the room and walked out into their rear yard, to stand and gaze at the stretch of lawn, the playground of the past.

Light rain was falling but she saw only the sunshine.

Tommy was throwing a ball to his father and laughing as he tumbled over when trying to catch its return; that vision came back, it was plentiful, never to be forgotten.

"I be a policeman when I growed up," Tommy said. "Stop naughty people."

"Yes, Tommy. That will be a good job for you."

"You be there, daddy, you never leave me."

"Never, Tommy, never. Daddy will never leave you."

And her husband, the down – to – earth Charles.

"Heaven is here, sweetheart. Here on earth. We make our own heaven, my heaven is here with you and Tommy."

Then the scene passed and the lawn was bare and the rain falling.

She returned to the house, and the chairman spoke to her, "I'll take care of everything," he said.

"Thank you."

She walked out to the front, down the path and into the street, to later find herself on the garden seat that she'd shared with Charles on their first meeting; knowing that never again would she sleep within the walls of that home, that paradise, that heaven of Charles.

"Pardon me," she said to Charles, glancing sideways towards him as she stood to leave.

"Will we meet tomorrow?" he asked.

"Yes. And the day after that. And the next and the next and forever."

But he was not there, she had seen him and heard him but he had vanished into her mind; locked into the memories of both joy and pain.

Charles stirred in his sleep, alarmed.

Her breath was coming fast and sharp, like a panting animal.

His hands slid across her chest, touching her heaving breasts.

What was it?

God. Surely she wasn't taking a fit. She'd never been the hysterical type. Too much in command for anything like that.

What had they eaten. Nothing unusual.

He reached for the switch to the bedside lantern, then paused. He mustn't panic.

289

Her fingers reached up to hold his hand. The grasp was tight. Why? So often had she taken his hand if it were down by her waist, to lift it up and spread it over a breast before she'd held it there. As if to say it is yours as much as it is mine. We share it. We share everything. Don't we? Isn't that what love and affection are all about? The sharing of both pleasure and pain.

Her body was wet. Perspiration. He felt it trickle across his wrist.

He would have to switch the light on, but to do so was a need to break her grasp and he had no desire to do that.

She was uttering something now. "Dear God, dear God, dear God. Oh, Charles."

That damned religion of hers.

Her free hand came up and he felt her body stiffen as her fingers traced the contours of his face.

"Who? Who is it?" she said.

He tried to laugh. "It's me, sweetheart. Have you been playing the field?"

They were foolish words. He knew. And strained rather than jesting tone.

"Charles. Is it You?"

"Of course it's me."

"And we are in heaven?"

"Of course, we're in heaven. I told you that before. We've made our own heaven, sweetheart. Just you and Tommy and me."

"And we aren't dead?"

He kissed her hair, tasting the salt of heavy perspiration that had stuck some of her hair to her face.

Her eyes seemed to gleam in the darkness of the room.

"Not dead, sweetheart," he replied.

It was crazy talk but he couldn't destroy it with ridicule. There was an urgency in the tone of her voice.

"And Tommy is still with us?"

"Of course, he's still with us."

"Please..... turn the light on."

"I can't. You're holding my hand."

She eased her grasp of him and he stretched to switch the bedside lamp.

Her face was ghostly white, near to frightening.

"You've had a nightmare," he said.

She pulled at the looseness of the bed sheet, to wipe her face.

"Did you go to Katoomba, Charles?"

"Yes."

"And the pills?"

He forced a laugh. "What pills?"

"That army man. You told me about him once before. You met him at a function. He was a friend of the manager at work."

"The colonel?"

"Yes."

"You're thinking of the suicide pills?"

"Yes."

"What about them?"

"Didn't you go up to see him about getting some. You said for a dog, and we haven't got a dog."

He laughed openly, somehow relieved.

"So that's why you were so upset. You thought I was going to put one in your tea."

"Not mine."

He laughed again. "My own?"

"Yes."

"Sweetheart, you're soaking with perspiration, and you've had a crazy dream...... Have a shower and I'll make the tea. The NO PILLS tea."

"You're saying that there weren't any pills."

"Yes, in the army. Not here in civilian life. I think they had to be returned to the quartermaster or somebody when back in base."

"Then why did you go up into the mountains to meet that colonel?"

"He had retired from the army and had spoken about opening a branch up there for the firm. An agency."

"And the doctor. Taking Tommy to the doctor. The school photograph. That was real."

"Yes." We did get Tommy's eyes checked. That specialist saw a slightly different sheen to Tommy's eyes and thought it better to be sure that sorry. It was your own idea. You recalled something about a distant relative in England."

"And Tommy's OK?"

"On top of the world."

"Dear God." She wiped a sniffling nose across his pyjama top. "So I created a rotten dream out of fear."

"It seems like it. You'd better tell me more if it'll make you feel better."

"No, no, no more. I'll spend the rest of my life trying to forget it." She lifted her face to look down at him. "So that's why God wouldn't let me have a second child."

He pulled her head down to his chest. "Oh, come on, sweetheart, please."

"No. It's time," she persisted. "It all comes back to me now. The real life things in that dreadful nightmare. It was God's way of telling me how painful life could be, if we had a second child...... the way that genes carry forward, both the good and the bad."

He ran a hand through her soakened hair. "Well, there should be better ways of passing the message other than frightening the hell out of me...... and yourself."

"No, Charles, please. You don't understand."

"That's true," he said with a grimace. I'll make us some tea."

"No. I will after I shower."

"You'd better come back naked so that I can shake some sense into you."

"I intend to, if you try to understand the dreadful experience I've just had that ended so beautifully."

"Beautifully? There must have been a man in it."

"There was...... you." She had clambered from the bed and was looking down at him. "You were wonderful."

"That makes sense." He smiled as he spoke, trying to soften the fright from her quickened breath that had not fully recovered.

"Could you believe that five years of a person's life could flash through a mind in one night? A dream."

"So that's what shook you up. It was something about Tommy. He's five years old now."

"Yes."

"Tell me." He clasped her nightdress.

"No. Never."

"Well, to answer your question, I'll say yes."

"What question?"

"About things flashing through a mind in a dream."

"Oh, I wasn't thinking of it as a question."

"Well. I'll answer it, anyhow."

"How can you answer it?"

"Something I read years ago. I didn't believe it till now." He was pulling harder at her nightdress. She knew why and she felt her body relax.

"Tell me. If it makes sense."

"You decide. After I tell you. What I read years ago was that a man and his daughter were both pilots of small aircraft. The father brought a new two seater plane and took his daughter for a joy ride. Playing the fool a bit, I suppose, and thinking that his daughter had strapped herself into the security harness, he flew the plane for a while upside down."

"What happened?"

"He glanced over his shoulder and the rear seat was empty. His daughter hadn't bothered to secure herself."

"Good Lord."

"Yes. Good Lord it was."

"You're having a shot at me about my religious views."

"No. The opposite, sweetheart, so let me finish the story."

"Only if it doesn't make me cry."

"It was in Europe and there had been heavy snowfalls. The girl who fell out ..... about two thousand feet up, they say, came down onto one of those leafy fir trees that was buried in piles of snow."

"And?"

"They fished her out and gave her a hot shower and a cup of tea."

"You made that up."

"No. It was a true story."

"So why did you tell me now? If you let my gown free I'll freshen up."

"I told you now, because when that girl was interviewed.... the one who fell out of the aeroplane, she said that, as she fell, all of the important things in her entire life, flashed through her mind. Everything since childhood."

"Good Lord."

"Nobody believed her."

"I believe her. No matter what she said."

"So do I now. After what you've said."

He pulled harder on her gown and she toppled onto him.

"I need a shower, Charles."

"Let's both need it."

"I think I can hear Tommy."

"I think you're nice and slippery."

"You're dreadful."

"Am I that bad."

"Dreadfully wonderful. Will you come to church with me one of these days? You must believe in something now."

"I'll have to get Tommy's permission."

"He'd love you to come."

"He loves to come home."

"Because you're here."

He hesitated. "OK. Once a month."

She kissed him.

"No more nightmares, sweetheart."

"I promise. I've received a message and know what to do now."

He felt her breasts tighten within his hand. He also knew that fixed views could often be so wrong.

And, once again, she knew the wonders of life that she'd dreamt had been taken away from her had returned by the invisibility of faith....... and she cried and cried with joy as he ran one hand gently across her back.

The preceding story was written in a manner that should make most readers hate it because it depicked a mental scene that could have been part of their own lives........ either as the parent or the child.

But why should that happen in an educated world?

Or do we really live in an educated world?

Scientists fly up and check the moon for mushrooms, then return to earth as heroes.

The cost of that trip could have fed every starving person on earth for a month or a year or a life time.

Why have the flood gates opened for women to suffer breast cancer?

And men prostate cancer?

We know that genes have a lot to do with our health problems. But what creates our genes?

Is it the food our forefathers ate when they lacked mobility and were confined to a small area of land for their entire lives, and, accordingly, forced to eat from that land.

Blood is the by – product of our food.

I wonder if any statistics have been taken on the past origin of people, taken blood groups and their diseases and their eating habits?

Many years ago, I read that blue eyes are noticeably 'better' than other colours. Why? Are they? No answer.

In a bizarre way, we are made out, of food, aren't we? We certainly wouldn't make old bones without it.

So what causes this devastating eye problems in the newly born.

Are there more cases of it recorded to the lesser developed?

Does it flow through the blacks as often as the whites...... or more often? Or does anybody care?

And why did I not know that it existed until a neighbour working in that field drew it to my attention when I sought her knowledge?

Simple answer to that question. No money for that research. It's mushrooms on the moon that we are after.

P.S. Retinoblastoma. How could you forget it if you knew it.

F.A.H.

World Vision

There's been many a year
When I was tempted to say
Forget it, it's too much
Let's just go away
That crowds all a – bustle
With faces so taut
Heaped bags full of shopping
Arms straining, so fraught

The children all clamour
For the latest new toy
Only to find
Just an hour of joy
Then it's thrown to one side
And with eyes all aglow
They're looking ahead
To the next thing on show

I saw in the paper
A story, so grim
Of starving, sad children
My eyes filled to the brim
What did these kids know
Of presents and fun
Their lives such a struggle
Their teacher, a gun

It just isn't right
That we have so much
When children are starving
Our hearts it must touch
So when someone asks you
"What shall I give?"
Tell them "Donations"
So these kids can live

By Sharon Everson

Printed in the United States
by Baker & Taylor Publisher Services